Something Wasn't Right

As I was turning to the second tank, something at the edge of my vision caught my attention. I felt a mental tug, a message from my brain telling me to look again, that something wasn't quite right.

I turned back to the first tank and cried out in horror.

What I had seen was a man, floating face down in the chemical soup.

For an instant I couldn't move. I just looked from side to side, as if I were expecting somebody to step forward and take over.

But there was no one else in the room. I was alone with the dead body.

OMNI
SPACE STATION ICE-3
BRUCE COVILLE

SCHOLASTIC INC.
New York Toronto London Auckland Sydney

For my brother, Brian,
Who has always had his head in the stars

ISBN 0-590-40278-1

12 11 10 9 8 7 6 5 4 3 2 1   7 8 9/8 0 1 2/9

Printed in the U.S.A.

First Scholastic printing, November 1987

1. Trouble in the BS Factory

If the dead man in the waste converter had really existed, I never would have gotten into this whole mess.

But he didn't. At least, not as far as ICE-3 records went.

So I did.

Get in trouble that is.

My name is Rusty McPhee (actually, it's Edward, but everyone calls me Rusty, on account of my hair) and ICE-3 is where I live. The ICE stands for "International Colonization Effort"; the "3" indicates that this is the third colony to come on line.

You're probably wondering why I'm telling you all this. I mean, *everybody* knows about the ICE colonies, right? Well, maybe. But my grandfather, who's been writing science fiction since the 1980's for heaven's sake, keeps reminding me that just because we all know something now, it doesn't mean people will know it ten years from now. He says I should never underestimate the human capacity for ignorance, and if I want people to read this book ten years from now, I'd better make everything clear.

So bear with me while I fill in the details.

Actually, Gramps is the reason I'm writing this down at all. He keeps telling me he would have given his eyeteeth to have lived through something like this when he was a kid. My usual response to that comment is that it's a lot more fun to read about something like this than it is to experience it.

Anyway, the whole thing began on June 27 of this year. (2018, for those of you reading this sometime yet to come.) School had closed for semester break the week before, but my mentor program, which is where I'm getting my real education, was still going on. So early that day I signed out a two-seat Space Scooter from ICE-3 and flew over to the small Bio-Science Lab orbiting nearby.

The Bio-Science Lab (known affectionately to ICERS as the BS Factory) was headquarters for my mentor, Dr. Antoine Twining, whose research required special low-gravity conditions.

I had only been flying solo since I turned sixteen, two months before, and I still wasn't entirely comfortable piloting the scooter by myself. As I drew close to the lab I stuck the tip of my tongue between my teeth and bit down lightly. (It's a family trait, according to my mother; she claims every McPhee male does it when concentrating.) At first I wasn't even aware I was doing it — primarily because my entire attention was focused on the absurdly tiny docking space in front of me.

Docking a two-seater isn't actually that hard. But the maneuver wasn't second nature to me yet, so I was trying to be extra careful.

Unfortunately, I wasn't quite careful enough. I made a slight miscalculation, and the front of the scooter struck the right edge of the port. (The bump made me bite down, which was when I realized I was sticking out my tongue — primarily because I bit it.) I muttered angrily and waited as the scooter bounced gently off one side of the entryway, then the other, before finally stabilizing in the center of it.

I was really disgusted with myself. The bump wasn't going to cause any damage. But I was certain whoever was inside monitoring my arrival would be smirking at the error — laughing about "kid pilots."

I hate it when older people are condescending.

As soon as I was in position, powerful magnetic guidelines drew me into the BS Factory. Once the scooter had made it through the port, the door irised shut, closing out the void behind me. A moment later, I felt the scooter being lifted to press against the top of the air lock. When the door seal was in place, I pressed a button. The top sprang open.

"Nice landing, Russ," said Millicent Carter as I stepped out of the scooter. "Remind me to have you give my kid driving lessons next year."

I smiled. "No problem, Mill," I said. "Heck, you'll probably get an insurance rebate when they find out who you hired."

I didn't mind this kind of teasing when it came from Millie. A tall, good-looking, middle-aged woman, she was the kind who could let you know she was laughing with you instead of at you — even while she was dumping all over you. Millie was pretty much in charge of the Bio-Science facility. She wasn't a scientist, or an administrator, or anything fancy like that. She was just the one who kept things working.

"Where's the Doc?" I asked her.

"He's in his lab," said Millie, *"waiting for you."*

I heard the emphasis on the last words and sighed. It seemed like no matter how hard I tried, I couldn't manage to get here — or anywhere else — on time. I stepped into the hallway and began trotting along the curving outer wall of the substation, using the careful space jogger's technique that kept me from bouncing up to the ceiling in the lab's reduced gravity. Outside the door to Dr. Twining's laboratory, I grabbed one of the loops sticking out from the wall to slow myself down.

I was about to go bursting into the room, full of apologies for being late, when I pulled myself up short. I could hear Dr. Twining arguing with someone.

Things sounded pretty tense. I decided that late or not, I had better hold my horses.

The door muffled the angry voices enough so that I couldn't hear what was being said. But after a few minutes I was able to recognize the other speaker. It was Pieter Durkin. Like Dr. Twining, Dr. Durkin was one of the BS Factory's seven senior scientists. (Millie and I referred to the group as "The Mad Scientists' Club.")

I felt bad that they were arguing. Dr. Durkin and Dr. Twining were both fine scientists. And they had both been very good to me.

The voices got louder. Suddenly the door was flung open, and Dr. Durkin came storming out. He was carrying a chimpanzee in his arms, and his usually pale skin was flushed with anger.

"Hello, Rusty," he growled. Then he ran a hand through his thinning blond hair and tried to smile, as if he realized whatever was bothering him wasn't my fault. "Sorry to intrude on your lab time," he muttered. He lowered the chimp to the floor and hurried off down the hall.

The chimp, who was named Ron, turned and signed a little message to me: "Got to go. Bye-bye."

"Bye-bye, Ron," I signed back. I smiled as I watched him scurry down the hall.

Ron was one of my best friends; if nothing else, I could always count on him for a smile and a hug, which is more than you'll get from some people.

I stood in the hall for another minute or so after they left, figuring it wouldn't hurt to give Dr. Twining a little more time to cool off.

"Sorry I'm late," I said, when I finally thought it was safe to go in.

Dr. Twining stood at a lab table, his tall, gangling frame huddled over whatever he was working on. When he answered me his voice was almost unnaturally calm. "It's all right, Rusty," he said, without looking up from his work. "Actually, I've gotten so I count on your being late. It was nice to know I would have the twenty minutes I needed to finish this experiment without being interrupted."

Obviously, we weren't going to talk about his fight with Dr. Durkin. Well, that was his privilege.

I crossed the room and peered over Dr. Twining's bony shoulder. "More limb regeneration?" I asked, looking down at the mouse he was examining. The poor thing had three good legs and a bud where the fourth should be.

Dr. Twining rubbed his long, thin nose and nodded soberly. "Between the low-gravity effect and the improved hormones we're learning to generate up here, I think we might actually crack this thing before long."

I nodded back. I was well aware that even though the prosthetic device Dr. Twining wore at the bottom of his left leg worked nearly as well as the real thing, he continued to dream of growing back the foot he had lost in an earthside car accident some twenty years back.

I had a personal interest in his research myself. I've got a bum hip, a problem I was born with. Right now it doesn't do more than slow me down once in a while. But my doctor has told me I should plan on having it replaced sometime before I'm thirty. If Dr. Twining pulls off his research I might be able to have a real one. If not, I get to carry around a chunk of stainless steel for the rest of my life. The idea doesn't thrill me.

I waited in silence while my mentor finished examining the mouse. After a moment or two he sighed. Scooping up the small bundle of fur, he returned it to the cage at the end of the table. "Ready to go to work?" he asked.

I nodded eagerly. My sessions with Dr. Twining here in the Bio-Science Lab were the highlight of my day.

Within a half hour I was studying a slice of frog brain through an electron microscope, so lost in the mysteries of chemical information storage that I didn't notice Dr. Twining standing behind me until he tapped me on the shoulder. "I'm going back to the main wheel now," he said. I saw a smile twitch at the corner of his lips. "I'm meeting with one of my private patients: Dr. Puckett."

He waited for me to react.

I did. Elmo Puckett was the most famous man in ICE-3, a fabulously rich recluse who had invented nearly half the technology that had made the colonies possible. Everybody had heard of him, but I didn't know anyone who had actually seen him. According to rumors, he had huge private quarters in the center of the colony, where he kept his fingers in as many pies as possible. He never allowed himself to be photographed; any interviews I had seen only showed his hands.

"I didn't know you knew people like that," I said, after the shock wore off.

"Old friends from earthside," said Dr. Twining. "Elmo likes to paint himself as a hermit, but the truth is he knows more people than anyone I've ever met."

He glanced at the clock on the laboratory wall and changed the subject. "I want you to make sure you're not late for your job today. They tend to blame it on me when you are."

I promised and turned back to my work. In seconds I was so absorbed I barely heard the door close behind me.

By the time I looked up again, two hours had passed. I spotted the clock out of the corner of my eye and slapped my forehead in disgust. Despite Dr. Twining's request, I was going to be late. Again. I packed away my materials and dashed back to the loading dock.

"In a hurry?" asked Millicent.

"Don't bug me, Millie, or I'll teach your kid to drive backward. Just get me out of here."

"Hey, calm down," said Millie. "The scooter's all set to go. I was pretty sure that when you finally got here you'd be in an almighty hurry."

I relaxed. "You're a pal, Millie," I said. "Those driving lessons will be on the house."

"The way you drive," said Millicent, "they'll be on the walls, and on the roof, and — "

"All right," I said, hopping onto the scooter. "Just open the door and let me out!"

2. The Most Disgusting Thing I Ever Saw

The great wheel of ICE-3 floated in the blackness ahead of me.

I've pretty much grown up in space, so the colony is an everyday sight for me. But I always get a kick out of the way newcomers go on and on about the wonder of seeing the thing just hang there with nothing to support it.

The funny thing is, while they don't seem to have any trouble with the colony itself — it's OK for a world, even a miniature one, to hang in space — the mirror drives them crazy.

Like the colony, the mirror is nearly three and a half kilometers across. Unlike the colony, which consists of a tubular outer rim, an inner hub, six large connecting spokes, and a long outthrust spindle used for docking and mechanical purposes, the mirror is nothing but a simple trapezoid less than a centimeter thick. It reflects sunlight into the colony's interior.

The reason we don't take our sunlight straight is that it would fry us. While earth has a mile or so of atmosphere to soak up cosmic rays, there's no such luxury in an ICE Burg. So we shield the wheels with a thick layer of lunar debris to soak up the rays. Then we use the mirror to bounce sunlight in through a series of C-ray absorbing reflectors, so that by the time it gets to us it's no longer the kind of thing you'd wish on your worst enemy.

Anyway, because the mirror has no visible connection to the colony, earth-trained eyes can't help expecting it to either crash into us or just float away.

Beyond the colony, 240,000 kilometers away, floated the earth. Even though I was born there, I don't feel any homesickness for the planet. I hadn't lived on its surface long enough to develop any attachment other than gravitational.

My only regret about earth is that my grandfather is stuck down there. I think my life would be a lot more pleasant if Simon McPhee could be up here to act as a referee between myself and my parents. Besides, Gramps has dreamed of space all his life. He was thrilled that my folks and I could make it. But when I talk with him on the vid-phones, which is almost every day, I can see the longing in his eyes. He'd give his typing fingers to be up here with us.

Unfortunately, at this stage of the game everyone in the colonies has to pull his own weight and then some. There just isn't much need for an old-time science fiction and mystery writer up here right now. At least, not one who doesn't also have some kind of technical skill.

That's one reason I'm working so hard at my

education. I don't plan on being left behind like my grandfather. When the human race takes the next step toward the stars, I plan on being part of it. Biochemistry was Gramps's suggestion as a desirable skill for a starship crewmember. Fortunately, it suited my interests.

But that was a long way in the future. Right now I had to get back to the colony to do my duty at the Waste Treatment Facility — a job I had been assigned because the plant operated on biochemical principles. Skimming around the lunar debris, I headed under the torus.

(There is no real "under" in space, of course. But the adults have gotten into the habit of referring to the mirror as being "up." I guess since we get our light from it, it's too much like the sun they grew up with for them to do otherwise. Accurate or not, that leaves the other side as down, or "under.")

Docking at the spindle that extends out and "down" from the colony's center, I moved quickly to an elevator that would take me the half kilometer "up" to the Hub.

The six hollow spokes connecting the Hub to the outer rim of the colony, where most people actually live and work, are about twenty-five meters wide. To my relief, there was an elevator just ready to head out along the spoke closest to the Waste Treatment Facility. Better yet, it was an express. That meant there would be no stopping at the offices and labs along the way. Putting on a last minute burst of speed, I made the elevator, which traveled the kilometer out to the Rim in slightly over a minute.

Less than five minutes later, I had punched in my access code and was walking through the door of Waste Treatment, or the "Sludge for the Stars Factory," as my father insists on calling it. Actually, that name is highly inaccurate; nothing processed here ever makes it out into space. An ICE wheel is a closed system. We use every atom over and over again — primarily because the cost of shipping up new materials is so high we can't afford to waste a thing. That reality is so much a part of our daily life that "Waste not, want not" is almost a religion around here.

The time clock made a red slash across my card as I punched in — an indication that I was late again. (That information was instantly entered into the colony's main computer, of course. The red slash was strictly for my benefit, a kind of automated reprimand.)

"Your mentor called," said a mechanical voice as I crossed the room to get my white lab coat and gloves.

"Any message?" I asked.

"Yes," answered the voice. "Dr. Twining says he wishes you would learn to be on time."

I made a face and slipped on the protective mask I wear whenever I work in the treatment facility. The chemical banks we use to break things down are too powerful to take a chance on any accidental spills.

Wandering into the next room, I did a quick check of gauges. Everything was in order.

That didn't surprise me. The computer monitored the whole thing. I was just here as a safety measure, to guard against the system breaking down — an unlikely event, since it has two back-up systems to keep it going. I scowled as I made some marks on the chart on the wall. I don't like playing nursemaid to a virtually infallible machine. It's boring.

Turning to the holding tanks, I pressed a button and watched as the lid of one of them lifted. I had gotten into the habit of peering into the tanks to see what was being decomposed. I know, I know — it's disgusting. But it helps stave off the boredom. Besides, it fascinated me to see the stages of decomposition various things go through — especially in such a potent chemical situation. It reminds me of the time lapse films they used to show us in elementary science. You know, the ones where you see a flower blossom in thirty seconds. Only here the process was reversed. I wasn't watching growth, but decay.

Anyway, since it was largely a biochemical process, I could always tell myself it was professional curiosity.

Making sure that my mask was secure, I peered into the tank. Nothing very interesting — just the usual mixture of kitchen scraps and waste, slowly rolling over in response to the giant paddles rotating at the bottom of the tank.

As I was turning to the second tank, something at the edge of my vision caught my attention. I felt a message from my brain telling me to look again, that something wasn't quite right.

I turned back to the first tank and cried out in horror.

What I had seen was a man, floating face down in the chemical soup.

For an instant I couldn't move. I just looked from side to side, as if I were expecting somebody to step forward and take over.

But there was no one else in the room. I was alone with the dead body.

Finally, I ran to get a gaff hook, so I could try to pull the body out of the tank.

But when I returned to the edge of the tank, I caught my breath and fell to my knees. The action of the paddles had rolled the body over. The man's features were blurred by the action of the chemicals on his skin. His eye sockets were hollow.

The sight was too much for me. My stomach began turning and violently emptied itself.

I began staggering, and my foot slipped sideways. It pulled my bad hip with it. I cried out in pain as I crumpled to the tile floor. Then I was silent. At least, I assume I was, since I went out cold.

Oblivious to my troubles, the paddles in the tank drew the dead man back into the devouring chemicals.

3. Witness for the Decayed

When I first woke, I was too disoriented to think clearly. I put my fingers to my forehead, which was bleeding slightly from the smack I had given it.

At least that took care of the question of what to do first. Hobbling to the shower, I stripped off my clothes. Then I stepped in and turned the water on full force.

I yelped as the ice cold water hit my skin.

It was a cry of shock, not surprise. I *knew* the water would be cold. (You'd never use warm water for a chemical accident, after all — it would only speed things up.) But knowing and feeling are two different things. So it was still a shock.

But the cold water helped to clear my mind. Considering what was going on, I wasn't sure that was such a blessing. I might have been happier if my brain was still foggy.

Even after the shower I didn't know what to do next. I suppose if I had been on earth, I would have called the police. But we don't have a police department up here.

We never figured we'd need one.

After all, if you're going to put 25,000 people in a tin can in outer space and expect them to form a productive society, you're going to be pretty choosy about who you let on board. That's why every colonist selected for ICE-3 had been triple checked. First we were given a psychological workup, to see if we could withstand the pressures of living in space. Then the colonial administration used their computer to compare psychological profiles, to avoid "explosive personality combinations." Finally, the computer did a background check that was so thorough it could probably tell you embarrassing secrets about your grandmother when it was done.

The point is, if we didn't all get along perfectly, at least we were sure we didn't have any muggers or murderers on board.

Or so we thought.

That was part of what was so horrifying about finding that body. If I had been earthside, I doubt it would have bothered me so much. I mean, I get the impression that in some of the cities down there you're lucky if you can get through a whole day without tripping over a corpse.

But up here we never expect to see something like that. So when I found that body in the tank it left me feeling like my world had been turned on its ear.

My father used to have a sign over his desk that said Everything You Know Is Wrong. That was how I felt now. It wasn't a pleasant sensation. In fact, it was downright frightening.

"Get a grip on yourself, Rusty!" I yelled, grabbing my head and squeezing it. (Don't ask me what good I thought that would do.)

I closed my eyes and took a deep breath. That was more helpful. As I calmed down, I realized my first step should be to call Dr. Hadley, my supervisor for this job.

Unfortunately, Dr. Hadley wasn't available. And Dr. Twining had told me he would be tied up today.

Now what?

I decided to call the Office of Dispute Management. Even though this wasn't really up their alley, I figured they would be my best bet.

Dispute Management is the closest thing ICE-3 has to a police force, although the people who work there prefer to call themselves "Ombudsmen." I guess that's fair. Their work is more diplomacy than enforcement; usually they don't deal with anything more serious than two scientists squabbling over lab time. Still, their job was to solve problems. And a problem I definitely had.

I put through a call. A man with steel gray hair appeared on the tele-screen. "Office of Dispute Management," he said. "Can I help you?"

"I want to report a murder."

The man looked as if he had swallowed something that was still alive. And wiggling.

"What did you say, young man?"

"A murder!" I shouted. "I want to report a murder!"

The man looked angry. I guess people don't like having their day shaken up like that.

"If this is a prank . . ."

"There's a dead man in the Waste Disposal Tank!" I shouted. "Are you going to do something about it, or not?"

"What's your name?" said the man.

"What difference does that make?" I yelled.

"I have to make out a report."

I rolled my eyes in disgust. "Will you get somebody over here?" I said. "We can make out the report later. If we don't get that body out of the tank soon, there won't be anything left of it."

"Where's your supervisor?" he asked.

"I can't reach him."

"What do you usually do in case of an emergency?"

"We've never had one."

"Well, what would you do if you did?" snapped the man.

"If it was bad enough, I'd shut down the system."

"All right, if you're telling the truth, and there really is a body there, you'd better shut down the system. But if there isn't, you'd better be prepared to suffer the consequences."

"Thanks for nothing," I snapped. I slapped the off switch and took some pleasure in seeing the jerk flicker out of sight.

Then I went and shut down the system.

It wasn't long before I heard from my boss. The shut down had set off an alarm he carries with him wherever he goes.

"Rusty!" cried a voice from the ceiling, "what in Sam Hill is going on?"

"You'd better get down here quick, Dr. Hadley!" I yelled. "There's a dead man in tank one!"

He started to ask me a question, thought better of it, and said "I'll be right there!"

And he was, too. Showed up just about the time the guy from Dispute Management got there.

I really don't want to describe what happened next. Let's just say they both yelled at me. Then they started yelling at each other. Then they took turns yelling at me *and* each other. After a while someone got the bright idea of looking in the tank to see what I was talking about.

It was too late, of course. The body was gone — completely dissolved. They decided to drain the tank. It didn't do any good; there wasn't anything left of that guy that you couldn't have bought at your local chemical supply store.

"OK, lad, I think you'd better come with me," said the man from Dispute Management. His name was Dyvach Jones, and we weren't getting along any better in person than we had over the phone.

"What for?" I asked.

"A lot of things," said Jones. "I'll want a statement from you. We'll need a formal description of this 'body' you thought you saw. And I want to run a few blood tests on you."

I knew what he was getting at, and I didn't like it. "I'm not on anything," I said tersely.

"I'll vouch for that, Jones," said Dr. Hadley. "Rusty's not that kind of kid."

"They never are," said Jones gruffly. "But I happen to believe in Occam's Razor. And the idea that this kid has been sniffing, or popping, something one of his friends cooked up with their home chemistry set is a lot easier for me to swallow than that someone in ICE-3 is a murderer."

Dr. Hadley shrugged. "Have it your way," he said. "I'm sure you won't find anything." He looked at me, and I could see the question in his eyes: You're not going to make a fool of me on this, are you?

I looked straight back at him and shook my head just a fraction of an inch.

He smiled. "You better just do what he says, Rusty. It'll be easier that way."

I shrugged and headed out the door after Dyvach.

I figured at least this way I wouldn't have to clean up the mess.

Just shows you how wrong a guy can be. There's more than one kind of mess and more than one kind of cleaning up. I spent the next hour and a half trying to keep from losing my temper while Jones worked me over from six different angles.

I really don't think he ever believed my story. Even the fact that his tests didn't show a trace of anything but good old red cells and white cells in my veins didn't slow him down. All it did was change his theory. He decided that if I wasn't on drugs I must be pulling some kind of prank.

The last straw came when the computer check he had ordered on the current status of the colony came back to him. "Everyone present and accounted for," it said.

"What do you have to say to this?" said Jones, waving it under my nose.

I didn't say anything. What could I say? As far as I was concerned, the report meant one of three things:

1. The computer was wrong.

2. There was someone up here we didn't know about.

3. I was losing my mind.

All things considered, the third possibility was probably the least frightening. After all, we depend pretty heavily on the computer. We have a lot of backup systems, of course. But even so, it's a major part of our lives.

If the computer really had made an error, I could see three possible reasons:

1. There was something wrong with the computer.

2. Someone was tampering with it.

3. It was being fed faulty data.

Again, considering the degree to which the colony relies on the computer system, I didn't find any of those ideas particularly appealing.

What about the idea that there was someone up here we didn't know about? If there was, it had to be one of two people: the killer or the victim. Or maybe both. In any event, I didn't find the idea of someone sneaking into a closed colony 240,000 kilometers from the nearest planet all that reassuring. I began fantasizing that we had been invaded by some strange space creatures.

The brief daydream seemed to give a lot of strength to my third theory: I was losing my mind.

"Well," repeated Jones. "What do you have to say for yourself?"

Look, I hope by the time you've made it through three chapters of this thing you've decided I'm not totally stupid. (Though I suppose you may change your mind when you read about some of the mistakes I made in the next few days.) Anyway, I was never one to get a lot of pleasure out of banging my head against a brick wall. I decided I'd had enough self-torture for the day, dropped my head, and whispered: "I'm sorry."

Please note — I didn't say what I was sorry about, which was mostly that Jones was too stupid to see I was telling the truth.

At that point, I just wanted to get out of there. I figured I had wasted enough energy on Mr. Dyvach Jones, and it was time to take things into my own hands.

I had a phone call to make.

4. The Colony

It's about two kilometers from the Office of Dispute Management to our apartment. I skipped the rolling sidewalks and went on foot. I figured the exercise might help me let off steam.

And boy, did I need to let off steam. I was still boiling from the lecture Jones had given me *after* I apologized — a ten-minute tirade on foolish pranks and wasting other people's time. (I know it lasted ten minutes, because I timed it. If I was just going on the basis of how it *felt*, I probably would have said three hours. Or longer. It seemed like it would have outlasted one of those tasteful-but-endless British miniseries my parents are always watching on our wall screen.)

Even worse than Jones's lecture were the threats he made when he was done. All kinds of things about what would happen if I ever dared, blah, blah, blah, etc., etc., etc. . . . I'll tell you, it was a good thing I had already thrown up once that day. Otherwise his desk would have been in real danger.

Anyway, after I had meandered past a few of my favorite shops, my stomach began to remind me that it was now extremely empty. So I stepped into a fast-food spot.

Since we don't have the room to raise grazing animals, our primary meat source out here is the cuddly but rapidly reproducing rabbit. Which means our fast-food shops tend to specialize in things like the Double McBunny Burger.

I had two.

If you've never tasted one, stop laughing and wait until you've tried it.

Then you can laugh.

Actually, I kind of like the things. I'm certainly glad I'm not like my father; he's been known to get so desperate for a piece of beef he'd consider trading his mother to the first person who offered him a genuine steak in return. And he's not alone. One of ICE-3's biggest political controversies is whether or not we should use some of our precious land area to raise cattle. People have enormous fights about it.

Personally, I think it's an awful lot of fuss over whether or not someone gets to chew on a piece of dead cow every once in a while. Me, I'd just as soon stick to rabbit.

Once I had finished mine, I wandered out of the shopping area and into the Altair Park orchard, which took me to the base of our apartment complex. I stopped to sit on my favorite rock and enjoy the view.

I have to keep reminding myself of what my grandfather said — I mean, about not assuming you know what all this is like. The view from the rock is so natural to me it seems silly to describe it. But maybe you've never seen a picture of the inside of an ICE wheel.

If you haven't, hang on to your hat. This gets a little complicated.

The first thing you have to remember is that since we're too small to have much real gravity, we use centrifugal force to make a kind of fake gravity. An ICE wheel spins on its axis once every sixty seconds or so, depending on its size. That "throws" everything outward (swing a yo-yo around your head and you'll have the basic idea.)

What does that have to do with the view from my rock? Well, to begin with, it means once you're inside the colony, "down" is in the direction of the outside edge.

I know, from watching newcomers, that it's hard to get this straight. When you look at the wheel from the outside, with the mirror on one side and the spindle on the other giving you a sense of "up and down," it's hard to realize that people inside the wheel aren't walking on the "bottom," but on the *sides*.

Think of one of those exercise wheels they have for hamsters and mice. Now imagine laying that wheel on its side. And imagine that instead of the wheel turning, the hamster can run all the way around it. That's the way it is here. We can walk all the way around the edge of our wheel. And when I sit on my rock, I know there are people on the other side of the wheel, over three kilometers away, *with their heads pointing at me.* But they're not upside down, any more than I am.

You have to remember that while planet dwellers live on the outside of their world, we colonists live inside ours. Here the horizon curves up. When I sit on my rock I can see about 200 meters in either direction; then the view disappears upward, around the bend. If I start walking, I'll walk uphill all the way, no matter what direction I go. (That sounds pretty strenuous, but in reality the slope is so gentle you hardly notice it.) And if I walk about seven kilometers, I'll end up back where I started.

(Some people have a hard time with that. It drives them buggy to be able to walk around the world in just over an hour.)

Anyway, from my rock I could see a broad band of land, about 200 meters across. To my right was a large, parklike area filled with fruit trees. (It's important to have parks — but they have to pay their way.) The colony's air circulation system carried the sweet fragrance of the trees to where I stood.

Beyond the park was an area filled with small shops and restaurants, and beyond that was a science and research area, where I could see one of the six spokes. A silvery tube some twenty-five meters wide, it rose straight through the colony, drawing my eye upward, toward our "sky," where the light bounces in from the big mirror. A little past that, the horizon curved up and out of sight.

I thought it looked pretty neat.

But of course, it wasn't the view that was on my mind.

It was that body in tank one. Apologizing to Dyvach Jones hadn't changed the fact that I had seen it there. Something was terribly wrong in ICE-3. And since it didn't look like anyone was going to believe me, I was going to have to handle this on my own.

Well, not quite on my own.

I got up off my rock and went to make that phone call.

I fiddled with a dial on my desk. When the focus on my wall screen improved, I punched a long series of numbers into my terminal.

The "WAIT" message flashed on the screen. I settled in to do just that while the computer processed my call.

I felt better now that I was here in my own room, surrounded by my own things. I suppose that just goes to show that no matter how far we stretch out into space, we're still basically territorial creatures. At least, I am.

A bell sounded, and my grandfather's lean face appeared on the wall. His hair, which had once been as red as mine, was shot through with gray and white. His green eyes creased at the corners as he smiled a welcome. It was good to see him, and I appreciated again the in-expensive colony-to-earth communication system the ICE Corporation provides for us. It's just good business, of course — one of those little things they figure will help keep us from going buggy. Even so, I get a kick out of being able to call across space for less than it costs most people on earth to call across town.

"Rusty!" he said. "I didn't expect to hear from you at this time of day."

Usually I called Gramps later in the evening; his evening. Our days and nights are totally artificial. Fortunately for Gramps and me, ICE-3's time schedule is only a few hours different from his.

"I've got a problem," I said.

One of the things I appreciate about my grandfather is that he takes me seriously. "I'm all ears," he replied.

I told him what had happened.

He rubbed his hands together. "That's the most fascinating thing I've heard in ages," he said.

"It may be fascinating," I said. "But it's got me plenty worried!"

The grin he had been trying to control faded from his face. "Sorry, Rusty. You know how I love a good mystery."

"I love them, too," I said. "When *you* write them. But I wanna tell you, it's a lot more fun reading about some poor guy finding a body than it is finding one yourself."

"I see what you mean. And you can't get anyone up there to take this seriously? Have you talked to your parents about it?"

I didn't have to say a thing. I just looked at him.

"I see what you mean," he said. "Well, I guess you'd better go see Dr. Puckett."

My jaw dropped. I looked at him in astonishment.

"*The* Dr. Puckett?" I asked.

"Of course," said Gramps. "He's an old friend."

5. Dr. Puckett

Gramps called back during dinner to tell me that Dr. Puckett had agreed to see me.

Since rumor had it that the man chewed up research assistants for breakfast, the idea made me so nervous I could hardly settle down all evening.

I wandered around my bedroom, looking for something to distract me. I tried watching the news from earth, but it was the same old stuff: food riots in England, another notch up on the worldwide pollution index, and more whining from an increasingly powerful bloc of South American countries that had declined to participate in the original ICE-Pact and was angry now because the colonies were becoming successful and they didn't have any of the action.

I switched off the screen and took out one of my grandfather's books, the first in his famous "MacDonald of Terra" series. But even the swashbuckling space adventures of Lieutenant James MacDonald couldn't keep my mind off what was going to happen in the morning.

Finally I crawled into bed and spent some time using the meditation techniques my grandfather had taught me. They must have worked, because when my bed started shaking in the morning (alarm beds are great if you sleep like I do) I found myself trying to wake up — which meant I had actually fallen asleep at some point.

Two hours later, I was standing outside Elmo Puckett's office, trying to get up the nerve to go in.

Counting to ten, I took a deep breath and rapped on the door.

"In!" yelled a pleasantly feminine voice.

I opened the door and floated through. For reasons known only to Dr. Puckett, he had chosen to locate his office and living quarters in the colony's hub, where there was virtually no gravity.

It was supposed to be a privilege, but considering what a pain it was to maneuver under the circumstances, I thought it was more like a punishment.

I decided his choice of locations probably had to do with his research — which just goes to show you how wrong a guy can be.

"You must be Rusty," said the wildly beautiful woman who was floating in the center of the room. "My name is Dr. Chang. I'll tell Dr. Puckett you've arrived."

Dr. Chang — Helen, as she later told me to call her — had jet black hair, enormous amber eyes, and smooth skin the color of an almond shell. She flashed me a dazzling smile, left what appeared to be a test-tube full of blood floating in mid-air, and touched a button on her belt. A puff of air moved her gently toward the door at the rear of the office.

When she disappeared through that same door, I took the chance to look around the office.

I've never seen so many books in my life! Every wall was covered with them. And I do mean *every*. Since there was no gravity here, there was no need to have a place to walk. Obviously Dr. Puckett had decided that under the circumstances a floor and ceiling were just a waste of good space. So he had put bookshelves everywhere except in the spaces used for doorways.

I'm fairly used to null gravity situations, but this was a new one to me. It was weird to look up and see shelves full of books hanging over my head — especially since no matter which way I turned the situation remained the same.

I was just trying to make my way to one wall to look at some of the titles when Dr. Chang reappeared.

"Dr. Puckett will see you now," she said. I could tell by the look on her face she was somewhat curious about that. After all, part of Puckett's mystique is his inaccessability.

Without another word, she recovered her test tube. Using her air mechanism, she propelled herself through another door off to my right.

I was alone in the room. Dr. Puckett was waiting for me behind his door.

But getting to him was easier said than done. Unlike Helen Chang, I was not equipped with an air-pack.

I imagine I must have looked something like a wounded frog as I paddled myself awkwardly across the room. I stopped when I got to his door. Should I knock, or just go right in?

That may seem like a stupid thing to worry about, but when you're dealing with a living legend, you want to do things right. Feeling like an idiot, I floated beside the door, dithering over what was the best approach. Finally, I figured I'd rather be safe than sorry, and I knocked.

"For heaven's sake, come in!" bellowed a voice from the other side. "I haven't got all day."

So much for etiquette.

I took a deep breath and touched the sill. The door slid into the wall, and I pulled myself into the room.

Even my sometimes overactive imagination hadn't prepared me for what was waiting inside.

The center of the room was occupied by an enormous desk. When I say center, I don't mean the middle of the floor. Dr. Puckett's desk was in the true center of the room — which means it was floating midway between the ceiling and the floor. It was anchored in place by floor-to-ceiling cords that kept it from drifting too far in any direction.

Unlike the first room, this one was not totally covered by books. They only took up four walls. One of the remaining walls was given over to diplomas, citations, and photographs. The other was made entirely of glass and looked out onto the hub's popular null-gravity swimming pool, where about a hundred people were splashing around and alternating between floating in the water and floating in air.

To tell you the truth, I don't know if I really saw all that then, or if I just picked it up later. I do know that most of my attention was taken up by the man floating behind the desk. Dr. Puckett was the biggest man I had ever seen.

Dr. Puckett. How can you describe a man like Elmo Puckett in just a few words. He deserves a whole book. ("Book!" I can hear him snort. "It would take an encyclopedia to do me justice!" The annoying thing about statements like that is that they're true. It took me a while to realize Elmo Puckett wasn't a raging ego-maniac. He was just realistic.)

Anyway, the first thing you noticed about Elmo Puckett was his size. I found out later his height was just a centimeter shy of a full two meters. When you figure that he packed a hundred and fifty kilograms onto that frame, you begin to get the picture.

He had thinning white hair, his skin was very fair (though his nose was criss-crossed by a small highway map of thin red veins), and his eyes were a shocking, electric blue.

"So you're Simon McPhee's grandbrat," he said, shoving himself away from the desk.

The desk quivered, held in place by the anchor ropes. Dr. Puckett himself floated backward to the window, bounced off at an angle, hit another wall, and then, using one of the anchor ropes for a brake, came to a stop a few feet in front of me. It sounds simple. But if you've ever maneuvered in a null-grav situation you have an idea of how much skill it took to pull that off.

I was appropriately impressed.

"People call me Rusty," I said, putting out my hand.

"I can see why," replied Dr. Puckett, glancing at my carrot-colored hair while he reached for my hand. "I'd offer you a seat, but as you can see, it's not really necessary."

I took his hand. It was enormous, and mine almost disappeared inside of it. My eye caught a set of deep brown stains on his fingers.

"Tobacco," said Dr. Puckett, following my gaze. "I used to be a heavy smoker. Still would be, if I could find someone up here to grow me some tobacco."

I was amazed. Smoking is illegal out here, of course. But most people are so disgusted by the idea that the law is considered almost frivolous. I couldn't believe someone would actually *want* to do that.

"So, what's the emergency?" asked Dr. Puckett. He reached behind him, grabbed one of the anchor ropes, and flipped himself backward over the desk, managing to end up just about where he had started out. "Your grandfather, old coot that he is, was very mysterious when he contacted me. He tells me very good things about you, by the way. I'd chalk that up to prejudice but for the fact that Antoine Twining also speaks highly of you."

My heart sank. I had been counting on Gramps to clear the way for me by telling Dr.

Puckett what had happened. Would he believe the story I had to tell him?

I took a deep breath.

"I think there's been a murder in the colony," I said. Then I winced in anticipation of his disbelief.

"How delicious!" he cried, rubbing his beefy hands together. "That's the best news I've heard in weeks!"

"You call that good news?" I cried, shocked at his callousness.

"You misinterpret me, Rusty," said Dr. Puckett. "I don't mean it's a good thing to have happen. But it's certainly the most interesting thing I've heard in a long time. It's not a piece of good news, but good *piece* of news, if you take my meaning. Now, why don't you fill me in on all the gory details. Let's see if you inherited any of your grandfather's storytelling ability."

But before I could even get a breath to start, he interrupted me.

"Wait. There's a couple of people I want to hear this."

He pushed a button on his desk. "Helen. Cassie. I want you."

Notice — no "please" or "if you're not busy." Just "I want you."

It was like a fantasy in stereo. Within seconds, doors on either side of me slid open, and two incredibly beautiful women came floating into the room. The one on my left was Dr. Chang. That meant the one to my right had to be Cassie. She was about a half a head shorter than me, with shoulder length blonde hair that was tied back in a ponytail (less trouble in null-gravity situations). The look in her eyes, which were very large and very blue, seemed to indicate that she took everything quite seriously. It was balanced by a little quirk that pulled at the corner of her mouth, seeming to indicate just the opposite — that she saw everything as one enormous joke.

Other than the fact that she seemed to be about my age, she might have been the model for half a dozen of my grandfather's heroines.

I just didn't know there was anyone like her running around in the real world.

I glanced at Dr. Puckett. He shrugged. "It's awful, isn't it? I mean, if having one beautiful female scientist as an assistant is a cliché, then having two is just wretched excess. But good gracious, boy, if the colonial management is willing to indulge my fantasies, who am I to turn them down? Just don't tell your grandfather about this. He has a hard enough time with the fact that we're up here and he's not. If he knew what my lab partners look like, the jealousy would probably kill him."

"Shut up, Elmo," said Dr. Chang.

Dr. Puckett sighed. "Anyway, as you can see, it's not an unmitigated paradise. Now, why don't you go ahead and tell us your story."

I hesitated, half expecting him to interrupt me again. He didn't, so I launched into a recital of the terrible things that had happened to me the day before.

When I got to the part about all the trouble I had with the man from Dispute Management,

Dr. Puckett began to smirk. I slowed down, half offended, half confused.

"I'm sorry," said Dr. Puckett. "I was distracted by a stray thought." He waved his hand as though dismissing it. "Please, continue with your story!"

I did. Right up to the point where my grandfather had surprised me with the information that he and Dr. Puckett were old friends.

"I used to give your grandfather technical advice for his stories," said Dr. Puckett, sounding rather self-satisfied.

"Anyway," I finished, "he said you were the best man in the colony for me to contact about this mess."

"I'm the best man in the colony, period," said Dr. Puckett. "But we'll let that pass. Your grandfather's instincts were on target. The fact of the matter is, I'm probably the only person in the colony for you to contact. No one else would believe you."

"But why not?" I cried.

Dr. Puckett shrugged. "You're a kid."

I started to protest, but he waved it away. "I know everything you're going to say: you've got a license, you've been accepted into the mentor program, you're involved in genuine research. That's all very nice, but it doesn't make any difference. We're not talking about reality here, Rusty, we're talking about perception. And in the eyes of anyone who has any power here, you're still a kid. Whether that's fair or not is irrelevant. You just have to recognize it as a fact and move on from there."

"If all that's true, then why do you believe me?" I asked.

He spread his hands and grinned. "Because I'm smarter than they are!"

Helen Chang groaned. "Elmo, you're impossible."

"No," he said. "Just highly unlikely. But that's beside the point. The question at hand is, how do we go about solving this mystery. Any suggestions?"

"I'm sure you have several," said Cassie. It was the first time she had spoken since entering the room, and her voice had a slightly acid quality to it.

"What a sweet child," murmured Dr. Puckett. "Always comes in right on cue. Indeed, Cassiopeia, I do have suggestions. I just thought I would give my right hand persons a chance to go first."

"Fine. Then I'd suggest we turn this over to the proper authorities and get on with our real work," said Cassie.

I felt myself bristle. "Brilliant suggestion," I snapped. "We just leave some murderer wandering around up here while idiots like Jones pretend nothing has happened."

"Look, Buster," she said, her blue eyes flashing, "just because your grandfather happens to be an old chum of Elmo's doesn't mean the rest of us have to believe your hallucinations."

"Hallucinations!" I yelped. "Listen, you — "

"Children, children!" cried Dr. Puckett. "Let's not squabble. It offends my delicate sensibilities."

"You have the sensibilities of a warthog in heat," said Dr. Chang.

Dr. Puckett ignored her. "Now," he said, rubbing his hands together, "I suggest the first thing we should do is finish our introductions. After his story, I think you all know something about Rusty. Rusty, the stunning scientist of Eurasian descent to your left is Dr. Helen Chang. She has three things that make her of great value to me: advanced degrees from Harvard and the University of Beijing; a brilliant understanding of Materials Management and Environmental Biology; and a high degree of tolerance for my nonsense. The lovely young lady to your right, who is serving an internship as my research assistant, is named Cassiopeia Jones." He flashed me a wicked grin. "I believe you've already met her father — Dyvach Jones, the colony's director of Dispute Management."

If Dr. Puckett's desk hadn't been floating five feet in the air, I would have crawled under it to hide.

6. The System

Well, what do you do in a situation like that?

Apologize? ("Gee, I'm sorry, your father is an idiot.")

Grovel? ("Ohmigosh, I didn't realize. I'm so sorry. Ohmigosh.")

Bluster? ("OK, so he's your old man. He's still a jerk!")

Not feeling comfortable with any of those options, I chose to stammer. ("B-duh, b-duh, b-duh . . .")

It wasn't pretty.

Dr. Puckett finally came to my rescue — but only after he had let me swing in the wind for a while.

"Well, these little things happen," he said cheerfully. "The important thing is not to let them affect our working relationship. Now, if the four of us are going to work together to solve this mystery — "

"Elmo!" cried the beautiful Miss Jones. "You can't be taking this seriously!"

Dr. Puckett rolled on without stopping as if

she hadn't said a thing.

" — then we'll have to set aside our petty differences and act as a team. Helen, you will be my second in command. Rusty and Cassie, you will do the leg work. As for myself, I will do what I do best."

"You're going to annoy people?" asked Dr. Chang sweetly.

Dr. Puckett refused to rise to the bait. "No," he replied, as if it had been a perfectly innocent question. "I am going to think."

"Heaven help us all," muttered Dr. Chang.

Cassie didn't say a thing. She didn't need to. It was clear from the scowl on her face what she thought of this whole affair. "Now," said Dr. Puckett, "what are the three major strands in a puzzle like this?"

"Suspect, motive, and method," I replied at once, having been well trained by my grandfather.

Dr. Puckett nodded serenely. "Very good, Rusty. So, we start by asking ourselves: 'What do we know about these areas right now?' The answer, unfortunately, is: 'Not much.' If we discount Rusty, we don't have any real suspects. Neither do we have a clue as to motive. And if we assume that the victim wasn't still alive when he got tossed into that tank of acid — a fate I wouldn't wish on more than about a hundred people I know, most of them lawyers and politicians — we don't even know how the poor chap was done in. In fact, we don't even know who he was. We don't even have a body, for that matter."

"Sounds pretty hopeless," said Cassie cheerfully.

"Exactly," said Dr. Puckett. "Which is what makes this such a fascinating case. Otherwise I wouldn't bother with it."

"So how do we start?" I asked.

"By taking unfair advantage of my position," said Dr. Puckett, in a tone of voice that indicated he truly relished the idea. "Since I have Priority One access to the computer, we'll do a few searches that you wouldn't be able to accomplish elsewhere. First we'll verify what Cassie's father told you. Helen and Cassie, I want you to work on that. It will probably take a fair amount of time, even with our capabilities.

"While you're doing that, I plan to set Rusty up with a program that will help him construct an image of the person he saw in the tank. But first, I want him to fill us in a little on the structure of the Waste Treatment system."

"You mean how it works?" I asked.

"Not the chemical process," said Dr. Puckett. "I helped design *that*. What I want to know is how stuff *gets* there!"

"Well, most of it is carried in by pipelines that run from the buildings. There's a whole network of them between the colony's outside and the inside shells."

Dr. Puckett nodded. "Pretty standard stuff," he said. "But since it's clear our man was neither washed down a drain nor flushed down a john, he must have gotten into that tank some other way. Now it's possible somebody actually lugged the body through the streets and into the Treatment Facility. But I don't really believe that's what happened. They'd be too exposed. So the question is, if you wanted to get something as big as a human body into the system, what are your options?"

I stopped to think for a moment. "I guess you'd use one of the bulk collection points," I said.

"And how many of those are there?" asked Dr. Puckett.

"About a dozen."

"And where are they located?"

Well, you get the idea. That was the way things went for the next several minutes. The funny thing is, by the time we were done, I understood the system better than I ever had before. It wasn't that I learned anything new about it — I was the one providing the information. But Dr. Puckett's questions forced me to organize what I knew and to really think about how the system worked.

I'll spare you the details and just give you the important parts:

ICE-3 is divided into six sections, which are marked off by the spokes coming in from the central hub. Three of the sections are agricultural, the other three are for business and housing. Each residential section is paired with an agricultural section, and each pair shares a Waste Treatment Facility.

There were a dozen bulk drops for the business and farm areas in our sector. We also serviced three of the eight orbiting substations, including the BS Factory. Waste material came from the substations in large cannisters and was then ejected into tubes that conveyed it to the decomposition tanks.

While I spoke, Dr. Puckett tapped away at his keyboard, muttering to himself about "stupid design work," and "I really should have gotten involved in that."

"Oh, for heaven's sake, Elmo, show us what you're looking at," said Dr. Chang.

Dr. Puckett looked up. "Sorry, Helen," he said. "I forgot you were there."

Dr. Chang made a little snorting noise, which I took to be a comment on Puckett's manners.

Dr. Puckett touched a button and the back wall of the office, the one that looked out over the swimming area, went dark. Almost at once it was covered by a large schematic diagram of the Waste Treatment system.

"Thank you," said Dr. Chang primly.

Dr. Puckett grunted something that might have been "you're welcome," but probably wasn't. He fiddled with the computer for another minute, then turned his attention back to me. "Important question: how long do you think the body was in the tank before you spotted it?"

"I'd say not more than fifteen minutes."

Dr. Puckett nodded. "And what time was that?"

I grimaced. "I was supposed to report to work at noon. I was twenty minutes late. I had been there about ten minutes when I spotted the body. So it would have been around twelve-thirty."

"Last question: is access to the bulk drops open or restricted?"

"Semi-restricted," I said. "You have to punch in your personal I.D. to use one. But they don't require private passcodes, or anything like that."

"That's all right," said Dr. Puckett. "As long as people have to punch in a valid personal code, we can get a record of it. It's going to take a while to work through the timing on this, but I ought to be able to get a handle on who was using the system yesterday."

Cassie spoke up. "If someone really wanted to get rid of a dead body — and I'm not saying anyone did, because I still think this whole thing is screwy — but if someone did, is it likely he or she would have used a personal code? I mean, that would be worse than leaving fingerprints all over the place."

Dr. Puckett shrugged. "It depends on a few things. For example, if the body was deposited by someone who frequently uses the Waste Treatment System, there wouldn't be anything suspicious about it. If it was put there by someone else, the odds are they didn't use their own code."

Cassie looked shocked. "But you can't use someone else's code. They're secret.'

"Oh, don't be so naive," said Dr. Puckett. "Of course you can. It happens all the time. The thing is, ninety-nine percent of the time when someone's code number is abused, it's done by someone well known to that person. So this list may not give us our killer. But it will at least help us narrow down our search. Since we're starting with 25,000 suspects, that seems like a worthwhile thing to do. Now, man your battle stations. We've got work to do!"

7. Make a Face

I followed Helen Chang and Cassie out of Dr. Puckett's office, back through the book-lined waiting room, and into the compound's private research facility.

I was properly impressed. Space is at a premium out here (which is kind of ironic when you think about it), and while none of us are really cramped, we all have to make little concessions in the way we live.

I was beginning to find out that Dr. Puckett didn't make concessions. His lab was enormous, filled with banks of computer terminals, dozens of monitors, and enough equipment to make it look more like a supply house than a working laboratory.

"What do you do with all this stuff?" I asked.

"A little bit of this, a little bit of that," said Helen with a shrug. "Elmo has a lot of different interests."

Maybe being involved in this mystery was making me suspicious of everyone, but I had a feeling she was being purposefully vague. I pushed the thought away. The last thing I needed right now was another mystery.

Following her instructions, I stationed myself at a terminal and logged on. A moment later, when Dr. Puckett established contact with me, Helen moved away to work with Cassie on their own assignment.

Following Dr. Puckett's instructions, I quickly became engrossed in a program that was very much like a game. Later, when I described it to my grandfather, I learned that it was just a high-tech version of a technique police have used for decades: the composite picture. The way it worked was, I would select a facial feature — a nose, for example. Then the screen would display several noses, all sizes and shapes. I would study them and indicate the one that seemed most like the nose of the man in the tank. (Considering the condition of his face when I first saw him, this wasn't always easy.) I was surprised to discover that not only was the program helping me create a picture of the face, it was actually working as a memory jogger, helping me to see it more clearly and vividly in my mind.

After about an hour I had chosen a facial shape and filled it in with eyes, nose, and mouth. I began to get frustrated because, while everything looked about right to me, for some reason the picture just didn't seem to come together. Fortunately, the program had several fine tuning mechanisms. By fiddling with the appropriate dial, I could adjust things like the distance between the eyes, or the width of the nose. And if I didn't like the change I made, I could just turn the dial back, and the image on the monitor would readjust itself.

That's a lot easier than erasing and starting over on paper!

At one point I got bored. After saving the most refined image, so I could go back to it, I began playing with what I had done. First I enlarged the nose. I started out slowly, but it wasn't long before I had the poor guy looking a little like a pelican. Not a very respectful way to treat the deceased, I guess. But I figured it wouldn't really make that much difference to him anymore. After a while, I began playing around with his skin color, and then his ears.

I had this really wonderful lop-eared, blue-skinned creature on the screen when Cassie came up behind me and looked over my shoulder.

"So, that's what the poor guy looked like," she said. "Well, at least it shouldn't be too hard to find out who he was. There can't have been too many people in the colony with a face like that."

That was what she said. The underlying meaning, which was easy enough to read from the look on her face and the tone in her voice, was much simpler: "Mister, you are some kind of jerk!"

"I was just taking a break," I said lamely. "Here, let me show you what I've really done." I typed in a command to erase the embarassing results of my boredom, then pulled up the real picture.

"Well, at least that one looks *human*," she said with a shrug.

I was trying to decide if I should ignore her or scramble around in my head for some withering comment, when Dr. Puckett's voice broke the uncomfortable silence that was developing between us. "Meeting in my office in ten minutes!" he announced from a speaker somewhere in the lab.

(It was a bit of a relief, actually; I was having a hard time coming up with a withering response.)

"It shall be as you wish, oh great master who must be obeyed," answered Helen. "Come on, Cassie. We'd better tie up what we've done before we go face the next wave of Elmo-isms."

For a few minutes there was silence as we all worked to finish our assignments. I fine tuned the image of the man in the tank a bit and then ran off four copies on the full color printer. All in all, I thought they were a pretty good likeness.

I was just gathering them out of the printer tray when Helen tapped me on the shoulder. "Come on," she said. "It's time to face the living ego again."

Dr. Puckett was smiling as we floated into his office.

"I trust you have all had a successful morning," he said. "For my own part, I have performed brilliantly, a fact I assume will surprise no one. Helen, how did you make out?"

"Pretty much as I expected," said Dr. Chang. "Between us, Cassie and I were able to verify the presence of every one of ICE-3's 25,112 people."

"Splendid!" said Dr. Puckett, rubbing his hands together. "We're 240,000 kilometers out in space, in a closed colony where everyone is accounted for, and we have a dead man who can't exist — and in fact, no longer does. Do you realize that makes this the biggest locked room puzzle in history? What a chance for us to be brilliant! And how did you make out, Mr. McPhee?"

By way of answer I passed around copies of my composite drawing.

"Anyone recognize him?" asked Dr. Puckett, staring at the picture of the broad-faced, sandy-haired man I had given him. Cassie and Helen shook their heads.

"And what have you turned up, Elmo?" asked Dr. Chang.

"I'm glad you asked that!" exclaimed Dr. Puckett.

"I know," said Dr. Chang. "Providing you with cue lines was the top item on my job description."

I was beginning to realize that insulting Dr. Puckett was like throwing spitwads at an elephant. Even if you scored a direct hit every time, it really didn't make any difference. He rolled on as if Helen hadn't said a word.

"Through a complex process of elimination, I have managed to compile a list of the people who could have put that body into a bulk collection spot. This involved some complicated comparisons of collection schedules, delivery times, and log-on notations. But it was worth it. I have narrowed our list of possible suspects by 99.71 percent — from 25,112 down to 73. Not bad for a morning's work." He glanced at his watch. "In fact if we could continue at that rate, we could pinpoint our villain in the next 10.43 seconds. Unfortunately, like the man about to reach the ground after stepping over a hundred-foot cliff, we have now come to the hard part."

"I don't like the sound of that," said Helen.

"You're safe for the time being," said Dr. Puckett. "It's Rusty and Cassie that I'm going to put into action. I want you two to go out and start talking to these people."

"What are we supposed to say to them?" asked Cassie. "Do we just go up and ask them if they killed someone and dumped him in a collection unit yesterday?"

"No. You show them the picture Rusty worked up and ask if they know the person. Odds are they won't admit to it, even if they do. But if you're paying attention, you'll be able to get a sense of whether or not they're lying. That's why I want both of you to go out on this one. One of you will be showing the suspects the picture — the other will be watching their eyes when they first see it."

"But what do we tell them?" persisted Cassie.

"What do I care?" snapped Dr. Puckett. "Be creative. Tell them it's a school project. Tell them your sister spotted him eating a Bunny Burger, developed an unrequited passion for the guy, and is pining into an anorexic stupor. Drop a hint that we suspect he's the forerunner of an alien invasion. All I want you to do right now is get that picture in front of these people's faces. Now, here's the list, along with each person's work place and home address. See how many of them you can get to before the day is over. Helen, I want you to stay here for a minute. I need to talk to you about our other project. . . ." He looked up at us, as if he were surprised to see us still hanging there. "Well what are you waiting for?" he roared. "Get going!"

I glanced at Cassie. It was clear she wasn't too pleased about all this. But it was also clear that she had no intention of arguing with Dr. Puckett. She touched the button on her belt and headed for the door.

Fortunately, I had been fitted with a belt of my own while we were in the lab. I started after her.

Unfortunately, it takes a while to learn to use those things properly, and I bounced off the walls a couple of times before I finally made it through the door.

It wasn't what you would call a grand exit.

8. Cassie

When I finally made it out to the hall, the look on Cassie's face did nothing to improve my self-confidence. It reminded me of someone who's been forced to baby-sit for their obnoxious little brother.

"You think I'm crazy, don't you?" I said.

"I've already answered that question," she replied.

"Cassie, I swear to you everything that I've said is true. I know it all sounds crazy. It *is* crazy. But that's why it's so important. There's something weird going on up here, and we're the ones who have to figure it out."

She looked at me, and I could tell that she was actually surprised. "You're really serious, aren't you?"

"Of course I'm serious," I said, surprised by her surprise. "Why else would I be doing all this?"

"I've been trying to figure that out," she said. "To tell you the truth, I didn't really listen to what you were saying, once you had said all those stupid things about my father. I was too mad. I guess I thought you were trying to prove something at his expense."

I sighed. "I was sorry about that after I'd done it," I said, trying to be diplomatic without being dishonest. And I was sorry — at least that I had gotten her so riled up. Anyone would be. I mean, who in their right mind would want to have someone that good looking upset with them?

The conversation seemed to smooth things out a little. I don't mean we suddenly became best friends, or anything like that. But at least I didn't feel like I was walking around beside a human icicle anymore.

We got in an elevator and headed for the Rim. We couldn't really talk — there were too many people around to discuss the mystery, and even though Cassie wasn't actively hostile anymore, we still hadn't worked our way up to casual conversation. So I had to content myself with the view, which is pretty spectacular when the elevator first enters the Rim. Unlike the ride through the spoke, where there's not much to see, since it's enclosed to protect us from radiation, when you break through into the Rim the glass sides of the elevators let you look out over the colony. It's an entirely different viewpoint than I get from my rock, because you're still a couple of hundred meters from ground level when it happens. Unfortunately, the elevator is moving so fast you don't really have time to enjoy it. In fact, some people never even see it, since anyone with a weak stomach usually faces in, so they won't have to watch the ground rushing up at them. Me, I always thought it was kind of exciting.

"What next, Sherlock?" said Cassie as we stepped out of the elevator.

Ignoring her sarcasm, I consulted the list Dr. Puckett had given us.

"The nearest suspect is about three buildings over," I said, after a few minutes.

"I can hardly wait," said Cassie.

I suppose the first time is always the worst when you're doing something like this. At least, that's the way it is for me. The attack of nerves I suffered as we approached the first office on our list was enough to make me want to take the next ship back to earth.

We paused outside the door and I located the name, Dr. Debra Doyle, on the list mounted beside the frame.

"What should we say to her?" I asked Cassie, feeling a surge of panic.

"How should I know?" she snapped. "This whole thing was your idea; I'm only here because Elmo made me come. You do the talking. I'll watch her eyes."

Thanks for nothing, I thought. What made her reaction really annoying was that she was right. I had gotten her into this. There was no reason I should expect her to carry the ball for me.

Straightening my shoulders, I knocked on the door.

"Come in," said a warm, feminine voice.

I touched the button at the side of the door and it slid open. Cassie and I stepped through.

"Can I help you?" asked the smiling brunette sitting behind the desk. She seemed very nice; unfortunately, she was not Dr. Doyle, but only her secretary.

"We'd like . . ." I stopped. My voice wasn't working. I swallowed and tried again. "We'd like to see Dr. Doyle," I said.

"Can I tell her what it's about?" asked the secretary, still smiling.

"It's a school project," I said.

The secretary gave me a funny look, but she buzzed her boss and repeated the message. I watched as she nodded her head. I couldn't hear the actual answer because it was coming to her through a small plug she wore in her ear.

"You can go in," she said at last. "You're in luck. She's in a good mood today."

Wondering what the doctor's bad moods were like, I led Cassie through the door the secretary indicated, into a room that was almost buried in books and papers. I wonder what it is about some of these scholars that makes them insist on real books, which cost a small fortune to ship up here, instead of microfilms and computer storage, which are cheap and easy.

Dr. Doyle looked up from the book she was examining. She had a stern appearance, yet there was a hint of humor in her eyes that made me feel at ease. "How can I help you?" she asked.

And then this wonderful thing happened: I opened my mouth and words came out.

Now that may not seem like much, until you consider that up till now my mouth had felt like it was full of cotton balls. Suddenly I was not only talking, I was making sense. In fact, not only was I making sense — I was on a roll.

My grandfather had always told me that being a McPhee, sooner or later I would find that I had the Irish "gift of gab." I had pretty much given up waiting for it. And now here it was!

"We're doing a kind of experiment for this scientist we work with," I said, skating as close to the truth as I could. "It's a long story, and I can see that you're pretty busy, so I won't take up a lot of time going into details. Basically it has to do with identification techniques and information chains. All we really want you to do is take a look at this picture and see if you can identify it for us."

Cassie handed me the picture, and I passed it to Dr. Doyle. She glanced at it and shook her head. "Sorry, can't help you," she said.

"That's all right," I answered cheerfully. "In this study a negative response is as useful, statistically speaking, as a positive one. Thanks for your time."

And with that I was heading for the door, before the good doctor had a chance to say "baloney."

"Well," said Cassie, when we were back out in the hallway, "for someone who didn't know what you were going to say, you did all right."

"Unexpected inspiration," I replied. "Let's

just hope it holds out. Do you think she was telling the truth?"

"Absolutely," said Cassie. "I don't think that woman could lie if she tried."

Merton Thorpe settled his feet onto his desk and loosened the flap of his collar. "So, whadda you kids want from me?" he asked.

"We're looking for this man," I said, handing him a copy of the composite drawing. "Someone told me they thought he might have worked for you." Which was true; I had asked Cassie to say it to me just before we entered Thorpe's office.

The man glanced at the picture then handed it back to me. "Never saw the guy," he said. Then he kind of squinted a little and added, "What are you kids up to, anyway?"

"It's a contest," said Cassie primly and somewhat to my surprise.

Thorpe looked at her, letting his eyes linger longer than I thought was appropriate. "More modern education, I suppose," he said with a snort. "Well, sorry I can't help you. Better luck next time."

He swung his feet off the desk and stood up, indicating it was time for us to leave. That was fine with me. There was something about the guy that rubbed me the wrong way.

"Well, what do you think?" asked Cassie, once we were outside his office.

"He's a jerk, but he's telling the truth," I said.

"I agree. He didn't even bat an eye when he looked at the picture."

To my surprise, I was beginning to feel pretty

confident with this technique of watching people's facial expressions when they looked at the picture. It was hardly what you'd call a scientific method. But it seemed to work.

Besides, it was all we had at the moment.

"That's ten," said Cassie, as she crossed Thorpe's name off the list. "I don't know about you, but I'm about ready for some lunch."

"Sounds like a good idea," I said. "After all, we've only got sixty-three left to go."

Cassie groaned.

We stopped at the corner outside Thorpe's building, and I punched a couple of buttons on the pedestal that stood next to the walkway. A map and some written information appeared almost instantly. "Closest fast-food joint is that way," I said, heading off to our left. "McBunny Burgers, here we come."

"Speak for yourself," she said. "I never eat the things."

"Why not?" I asked, not realizing what I was walking into.

She made a face. "I don't like hares in my food."

I collapsed against a wall and stared at her in shock.

"What's wrong?" she asked, all sweetness and innocence.

I shrugged. "I was going to say I didn't know you had a sense of humor. Then I realized that after that pun I still didn't have any proof. I think maybe I liked it better when you were hardly speaking to me."

She ignored me and kept on walking.

When we got to the restaurant I went and found a table while Cassie placed our orders and paid for the food. (We have a custom up here that whoever mentions eating first, pays; it's not a bad way to deal with things, except when two stubborn people get in a contest and go hungry for hours at a time.)

We sat across from each other and spread the list out between us so we could plan our strategy while we ate. I thought about trying to play footsies with her, but decided not to press my luck. I mean what we had had so far was a slight thaw in the cold war, not a declaration of affection. Besides, I wasn't sure I wanted to get involved with a girl who was willing to make jokes like that "hares in my food" crack — no matter how good looking she was!

"There's only two more people we can see in this sector," said Cassie. "Then we'll have to move on to New Ithaca. Either that or start figuring out what we're going to do about the people we have to contact in the substations."

Substations!

"What time is it?" I yelped.

Without waiting for her to answer, I leaned over the table and glanced at the small watch she wore around her wrist.

I was late again!

9. Back in the BS Factory

I was still mentally kicking myself in the rear when I started docking maneuvers at the BS Factory. Not only was I late again, but I had also reinforced Cassie's impression of myself as a jerk — both by losing track of time and then by rushing off the way I did.

I don't know why I keep doing this to myself. You'd think anyone with an IQ higher than a turnip ought to be able to keep track of time.

But I can't even keep track of a watch for more than a week. I finally decided it was simpler (not to mention cheaper) just to ask other people.

I want to tell you, it's not easy being a scatter-brain.

I took some consolation in the fact that this time I docked the scooter without a glitch.

Millie applauded as I climbed out. "Definite step in the right direction, kiddo," she said.

"Thanks, Millie."

"And that's important," she continued, "since a journey of a thousand miles . . ."

". . . begins with a single step," I finished with a groan. "Have I really got that far to go?"

"No. I just like to bust your chops. Which I imagine Dr. Twining is also going to do, considering what time it is."

"Don't remind me," I said, rolling my eyes. Suddenly I had an inspiration. Millie wasn't on my list of people who had used the bulk drop facility. But if my living/dead man had been here, she might have seen him anyway.

"Do you recognize this guy?" I asked, digging the picture out of my pack.

She looked at it for a minute. "Looks kind of like Hank Smollin," she said finally. "That is, if you make room for a lot of artistic license."

I couldn't believe it. A score!

"Who's Hank Smollin?" I asked, trying to keep from sounding too excited.

Millie shrugged. "Just some guy who used to work here. Hasn't been around for six months or so."

"Who did he work for?"

"One of the Mad Scientists, I think," said Millie. "Why so curious?"

"It's part of a game some friends and I are playing," I said, feeling truthful.

I was trying to act calm. But inside I was shouting with delight. If I had dared, I probably would have hugged her. Finally we were getting somewhere!

"I'll ask around for you, if you want," said Millie. "I won't be seeing the whole gang today. But I'll check with those I do."

The woman was a gem.

"I'd really appreciate it, Millie. Might make my life a lot easier."

"No problem," she said. "Your chariot will be waiting when you get back."

I was humming as I headed for Dr. Twining's office.

Dr. Twining wasn't. "I know I've made light of your tardiness in the past, Rusty," he said as I came through the door. "But I have to tell you that it is getting extremely tiresome. I want you either to begin to respect *my* time, or else find another mentor." He wasn't just snapping at me out of momentary annoyance. His voice was very cool and controlled. It was a cold anger, if you know what I mean.

I really couldn't blame him for being upset with me. But I didn't think it was fair to go from treating my tardiness as lightly as he had in the past to suddenly being so serious about it. For a minute I thought about saying so, but I figured it would only make things worse. Instead I mumbled a hasty apology, got out my notes and equipment, and buried myself in my work.

This certainly wasn't the time to ask about Hank Smollin.

But no matter how hard I tried, I couldn't keep my mind on those frog brains. Millie's information that my disappearing corpse had once worked in the BS Lab had me much too excited to settle down and concentrate.

After a while Dr. Twining left the lab. I waited for a few minutes and then put away what I was working on. I went to the computer terminal at the back of the office, logged on, and then dragged up the personnel file.

I found records for everyone who had worked for Dr. Twining during the last two years. There was no Smollin listed. I wasn't surprised. I didn't really think Dr. Twining had anything to do with whatever was going on. But I knew what kind of reaction I would get from Dr. Puckett if I failed to follow up on an angle for sentimental reasons.

I was just logging off when Dr. Magon came into the room. A short, enormously cheerful man, Dr. Magon was my favorite of the seven "Mad Scientists" who ran the BS Factory. He had a flair for practical jokes that kept everyone hopping. (It hadn't amused everyone, but I still had fond memories of the time he slipped a new compound he had been working on into the staff coffee pot and turned everyone's skin green for a week.)

"Hello, Rusty," he said. "Is Antoine around?"

I shook my head. "He left about twenty minutes ago."

"Curses, foiled again," said Dr. Magon, shrugging philosophically. "Oh, well. If you see him, tell him I'm looking for him." He started to leave.

"Wait!" I said.

He turned back.

"There was something I wanted to ask you."

"Yes?"

"Did you ever hear of a guy named Hank Smollin?"

Dr. Magon paused. "Sounds familiar," he

said. "Smollin. Smollin. Didn't he used to work here once?"

It was so quick that if I hadn't been watching like a hawk I would have missed it. Just a slight lifting of the eyelids, a miniscule flaring of the nostrils. But it was a perfect demonstration of what Dr. Puckett had told us.

No matter how casual Jymn Magon was trying to act, I was convinced he knew very well who Hank Smollin was.

It was an interesting afternoon. Now that I had new evidence that my dead man really existed, and I wasn't just losing my mind, I began to feel more confident about what I was doing. *And* more justified in my actions. This investigation meant annoying people, intruding on them, stretching the truth. I found all that hard to do when somewhere in the back of my head there was still this nagging doubt that maybe I really had been hallucinating, that maybe nothing had really happened after all.

But I couldn't have created Hank Smollin's face out of thin air. And now that Millie had named him for me, and I had gotten that strange reaction from Dr. Magon, I was convinced I truly was on the trail of something important. I wasn't just trying to satisfy my curiosity now, or deal with an unpleasant experience. We were talking about a man's life.

All of which explains why I became considerably bolder after my conversation with Dr. Magon.

The next person I spoke to was Dr. Jefferson.

Virginia Jefferson was over six feet tall, a slender, elegant black woman with a ferocious intelligence and a cool reserve that I had never seen anyone shake. Her research involved the effect of null-gravity situations on the nervous system.

"Dr. Jefferson!" I called, when I spotted her in the hall on the way to her lab. "I was just looking for you. I've got a message for Hank Smollin, and I was wondering if you could tell me where to find him."

She paused. Was that a flicker in her face? I couldn't tell — both because I wasn't close enough, and because she was so cool she probably wouldn't have batted an eye if I had told her I had just found evidence that I was her long lost son.

"Smollin," she said, in much the same way Dr. Magon had. "Smollin. Seems as though there used to be a man by that name working here. Not for me, though. And I don't think he's around any longer."

"Oh. Well, thanks anyway. I'll ask one of the others."

I pushed myself down the hallway, feeling stymied. I had seen rocks with more expressive faces. I had to remind myself that Dr. Puckett had never claimed that watching people's eyes would be foolproof.

Dr. Durkin's lab was next in line. He wasn't there when I knocked, but I went in anyway. This wasn't totally out of line. Dr. Durkin and Dr. Twining worked together so often that I had gotten to know him fairly well. On a number of occasions I had helped him with some piece of research, or carried something over from our lab. Whenever I did, he encouraged me to just come right in.

I looked around, wondering how long it would be before Dr. Durkin returned. I was tempted to use his computer to check his staff records, as I had in Dr. Twining's office. But that really would have been past the bounds of acceptable behavior. I hadn't gotten quite that bold. Yet.

A sound from the far side of the lab caught my attention.

It was my old friend, Ron.

"Hey, fella," I said. "How ya doing? Where's Nancy?"

Ron was one of a pair of chimps Dr. Durkin was using for his studies on how to counteract the negative effects of living without gravity. Nancy was his mate.

Dr. Durkin told me the chimps had been named after a twentieth-century president who had cut the heart out of the space program's budget.

Right now Ron was sitting in the corner of his cage, looking depressed.

"Poor fella," I said, crossing over to him. "You must be lonely."

I was hoping that nothing had happened to Nancy. I was fond of both chimps, and I enjoyed talking with them through the limited sign language that they had been able to learn.

"Where's Nancy?" I repeated, this time signing it instead of speaking it out loud.

"Don't know," signed Ron. "Don't feel good."

My heart went out to the miserable looking chimp. I was just about to open the cage to give him a cuddle when Dr. Durkin stepped into the lab.

"Rusty!" he shouted. "Get away from that cage!"

10. One-Way Ticket

I jumped back as if I had just touched an electric fence.

"What's the matter?" I asked. I was annoyed with myself because my hands were shaking.

"Ron is sick," said Dr. Durkin, "and we don't know yet whether what he has is contagious or not." He paused and took a breath. "Really, I'm surprised at you, Rusty. You can see there's something wrong with that chimp. And you've certainly been trained not to approach a lab animal that's ill when you don't understand its condition. I know you and Ron are friends. But you know as well as I do that any animal's behavior becomes unpredictable when it's ill. What if he had bitten you? You could have become infected, too!"

I felt myself begin to blush. Dr. Durkin was right. Even if I didn't really believe Ron would ever bite me, what I had done was still pretty stupid. Even worse, in terms of my standing in the BS Factory, it was unprofessional.

"I'm sorry," I said. "I don't know what I was thinking."

Dr. Durkin took a deep breath. "Well, no harm done, I guess," he said. "You just gave me an awful scare for a minute there. Actually, I'm glad you're here. I've been wanting to apologize for the way I brushed past you in the hall the other day. I didn't mean to be rude to you. I was angry with somebody else, and you just happened to get in my path."

"It's all right," I said with a shrug. Actually, I didn't feel as casual as I was trying to act. I was fond of Dr. Durkin, and it had bothered me when he went rushing by that day. I hadn't spent time brooding about it. (That would have been almost impossible, considering everything that had happened since then!) But even so, the fact that he took the time to apologize now made me feel good.

"Just take it as an unwarranted salvo from the midst of a mid-life crisis," said Dr. Durkin. "By the way, if you happen to see Antoine, tell him I was looking for him." He paused. "Well, now that the excitement's all over, what brings you here?"

I swallowed. After my stupid mistake and Dr. Durkin's gracious apology, I felt lousy about not being completely straightforward with him.

"I'm trying to contact a man named Hank Smollin," I said. "Somebody told me you might know where he is."

"Hardly," said Dr. Durkin. "I fired him six months ago. What on earth would you want to talk to him for?"

"Uh — someone gave me a message for him," I said, trying not to sound too stupid while I absorbed this new piece of news. "They knew he used to work here and thought that I could find him for them."

"Why don't they just use the Directory?" said Dr. Durkin. "I can't stand people who are lazy like that. You shouldn't cater to them, Rusty. It just encourages them."

"You're right," I said. "I'm too easy."

Millie wasn't around when I got back to the landing area. But true to her word, the scooter was waiting.

I took a piece of paper out of my backpack and scrawled her a note: "Millie — You can stop asking around. I found out who Smollin worked for. Thanks for the help. Rusty."

I stuck it on her clipboard, which was lying on her desk, and climbed into my scooter.

Getting out of the BS Factory was a little trickier without Millie around. I had to go through a complicated set of procedures to activate the air locks. They were a pain in the neck. I didn't really mind, because they were designed to prevent careless errors that might cause some kind of major accident.

Pretty soon I was out in space again. I circled once around the BS Factory just to enjoy the view and then headed back toward the colony.

How can I tell you about being in space? When you're out there on your own, with nothing but a bit of metal between you and the void, it makes you feel incredibly tiny. Usually. Every once in a while, if I'm in a particularly good mood, just the opposite happens. I feel like I merge into it, somehow become a part of the whole thing, connected to all of it.

Then I feel enormous.

Sometimes the whole thing just makes my brain start to spin around. Especially when I get looking off in the distance. I'll stare at the stars and start thinking about how far away they are and about how some of the things I'm seeing aren't stars at all, but other galaxies, with billions of stars inside of them. And then that old question starts to rattle around inside me, the one about "It can't possibly go on forever — but if it does have an end, what's next?"

I got thinking that way now, and I didn't pay much attention to where I was heading. That's not usually a big deal. The scooters have a pretty good range, and if you go flying off course it's no problem to get back. In fact a lot of people use them for recreation — just going out for a ride to get away from the confines of the colony. But when I turned my attention back to what I was doing, I realized I did have a problem: the scooter wouldn't respond to my commands.

I twisted the steering mechanism.

Nothing happened.

I tried again, in the opposite direction.

Nothing happened.

I switched on the radio to call for help.

Nothing happened. At least, not for a moment. Then, without my touching anything, the scooter suddenly shot forward, its speed quickly doubling, then tripling.

That's when I finally realized what was going on: I had asked one too many questions in the wrong place. Someone was getting nervous — someone who figured the best way to get rid of me was by sabotaging my scooter.

This wasn't just an equipment breakdown.

It was another murder.

11. The Stars

The only part of my body that seemed to be working was my brain. Unfortunately, it wasn't much use at the moment. All it wanted to do was tell me what was going to happen next. Against my will, I imagined myself floating past the orbits of Mars and Jupiter and Saturn, on past the outer planets, out of the solar system, across the galaxy, into Deep Space, on and on and on, until I either crashed into a star (extremely unlikely) or space and time themselves finally came to an end. For one mad instant I consoled myself with the idea that at least I would finally get an answer to my question about the edges of the universe.

Then some spoilsport in the back of my head whispered, "A lot of good that's going to do a dead man, Bozo."

The words seemed oddly familiar. Where had I heard them before?

Suddenly I remembered. I had read them in one of my grandfather's books.

The realization seemed to jolt me back into action. What would my grandfather do in a situation like this? Or, more importantly, what would his great character, Lieutenant James MacDonald, do?

I had read Gramps's entire "MacDonald of Terra" series at least three times. The thing I admired most about the hero of the stories was the way he never lost his cool when he was in a tough situation. (Having always been inclined to do something stupid first and then try to fix it later, I thought this was a great trait.)

"OK, Rusty," I told myself. "Can the panic. Let's take a look at the situation and see if we can figure something out. Start by taking a deep breath."

I followed my own advice and was surprised to realize how long I had been holding my breath. I had been so frightened I hadn't realized my lungs were screaming for air. The inrush of oxygen almost made me giddy.

I sat quietly for a moment, trying to regulate my breathing, to calm myself enough so I could think.

When I was ready, I began to take stock of the situation.

It was clear that the scooter had been rigged to get rid of me. I suppose if I had been a mechanical genius I could have changed the programming and gotten myself back on course for the colony.

Unfortunately, mechanics and programming were not my specialty. There was no way I could change the course of this thing. I was trapped on a one-way trip to nowhere.

I thought about MacDonald of Terra again. His philosophy, which I guess was also my grandfather's philosophy, went something like this: if you can't go through the door, blast open a window.

Blasting open a window in this thing wouldn't do me much good.

Besides, I didn't need to blast open anything. The scooter had a spring-operated safety ejection system that didn't depend on the regular power source.

But considering the difficulty I had experienced trying to move even two meters in the null-gravity of Dr. Puckett's office, I couldn't see much point in trying to "swim" back to the colony from this distance.

That was when the answer hit me. When I had realized I was late (again) for my session in the BS Factory, I had left Cassie in such a rush that I hadn't bothered to take off the belt they had given me in Dr. Puckett's office. I *did* have a way back!

I looked over my shoulder. The colony was already a long way off — and the distance was increasing rapidly.

I had to move fast.

Tearing up the seat beside me, I wrenched out the emergency suit stored there. Even though I had practiced using it in order to get my licence, putting on the suit in the tight confines of the scooter wasn't easy. My knees and

elbows kept getting stuck in different places —
I was three inches taller than I had been when I
took the test. Trying to pull the space suit over
my shoulder while my knee was wedged under
the control console, I was struck by a vision of
myself dying in this position. I would float
through eternity this way, doomed by my own
adolescent gawkiness. It seemed both ridiculous
and terrifyingly possible.

And it made me so mad I was able to wrench
the suit into position, though I gave my bad hip
an awful twist in the process.

I put on the helmet, locked it into place, and
then strapped on the airtanks, which consisted
of three smallish cannisters welded together.
According to the directions printed on the outside, I had two hours worth of air. I looked back
again, and wondered if I could possibly make it
to the colony in two hours. With only the air belt
to give me impetus, I would head back a lot more
slowly than the runaway scooter had taken me
outward.

Trying to ignore my throbbing hip, I strapped
on the propulsion belt, which I had removed
before I tried to put on the space suit. Then I
began the series of operations that would free
me from the scooter. There were three separate
steps. (The idea was to keep klutzes like me
from accidentally blowing themselves into space
while traveling back and forth between the
colony and the substations).

I finished the sequence.

Nothing happened.

I screamed.

Wouldn't you? I mean, I thought I had just kissed off my last hope.

Even so, I felt pretty silly when I realized the only thing wrong was that I had performed the operations in the reverse order.

I tried it again.

Victory! The top of the scooter blew off and I could feel the rush as the air around me was sucked into space.

I went with it.

I was separated from the scooter. But my momentum was still away from the Colony. I had to change that, and fast.

I touched the propulsion belt and started slowing myself down.

Slowly.

Very slowly.

I thought about screaming again. I could see my home floating in the distance. Once I had myself pointing in the right direction I would eventually reach it. But I didn't know whether I would be alive or not when I got there.

What a helpless feeling! Using the belt at full strength, all I had done so far was reduce my outward momentum. I wasn't even heading in the right direction yet!

I gave the belt another jab. I had to be careful. Once I got going in the right direction I would still need the belt to correct my course. I couldn't afford to use up all the power now.

I focused my attention on the stars.

After a while, I began to think that even if I made it back alive, I wouldn't be sane. I began to feel a terror unlike anything I have ever known.

And then the vastness of what was around me began to sink in.

In reality, compared to the distances involved, I wasn't a hair closer to the stars than someone standing on earth looking up at them.

But when I turned the right way, there was no earth — no colony — no scooter. There was only me and the stars. Even now it makes tears well up in my eyes when I think about it. Not that it was so terrifying, though it was.

It was just that, I guess. Those last two words. It *was*. It all existed, and I was part of it. Me and the stars.

This sounds stupid. How can I possibly explain it to you? I felt like I was crawling over the face of the universe, and I was so tiny I was beneath notice — and at the same time I was so much a part of it that I felt like my body had come apart at the seams and thrown my atoms around the curve of space. I was less than nothing. I was enormous beyond belief.

For a time I don't think I cared whether I was going to make it back or not.

The moment didn't last. Shortly after I was swept away by all these cosmic feelings, a little beeper went off in my ear.

It was the suit, warning me that my air supply was starting to run low.

Life is weird. One minute you're convinced you know the secret of the universe. The next you're scared silly because pretty soon you're going to die for lack of a few cubic inches of oxygen.

12. Deep Breaths and Fast Spurts

I suppose if I learned anything from the following three minutes, it's that panic is not a useful emotion. At least, not when you're trying to think clearly. Every now and then I still thank whatever powers there are that no one was around to see how I acted when my fear was at its height. (I'm not about to describe it here, either. I've been very honest in writing all this down so far. But some things are just too embarrassing to share.)

Anyway, after a few minutes the panic began to ebb away, and I tried to take stock of the situation somewhat more rationally.

Do you want to talk about stupid? Try this one on for size: after all that agony, I realized I didn't have to find a new oxygen source. I had been wearing one all along.

Remember the triple cannisters of the airpack? (This is so embarrassing; just writing it down makes me blush.) The beeping I had heard was actually a warning that the *first* cannister was nearly empty. Since *each* cannister held two hours worth of air (not two hours total, as I had been thinking), I still had another four hours before I started turning blue.

The scary thing is, if I hadn't figured out what was going on, I would have suffocated anyway. Death by Stupidity — how's that for an awful way to go?

Despite the reprieve, the basic situation was as deadly as ever: I was a long way from the colony and unlikely to make it back alive.

All this brought about some interesting emotions. Realistically, I was just as likely to die as I had been five minutes ago. But the sudden discovery that I had another four hours to live, instead of just a few minutes, made the moment of doom seem days, even years away.

Basically, this made me very happy.

But it wasn't all good. A couple of times I thought it might be preferable just to get things over with. I mean, as far as I could tell, I was going to spend four hours floating slowly toward home, all the while knowing I didn't have a prayer of getting there alive. This would be followed by a few minutes of running out of air, followed by turning blue, followed by dying.

Frankly, it struck me as being a particularly grim way to spend the last 240 minutes of my life.

"MacDonald of Terra would never give up in a spot like this," I told myself.

MacDonald was always on the verge of death and getting out of it in some unexpected manner. It was his trademark. And while it would probably make Gramps angry to be called a philosopher, there was one message that came shining through in all his books: where there's life, there's hope.

Most critics think this is pretty sappy. That might be so. Sappy or not, it helped keep me sane out there.

But what saved my life in the long run was interchangeable parts. That, and a little idea that was so clever it still makes me smug when I remember it.

I might not have gotten the idea if it hadn't been for the next disaster, which occured when my belt ran out of power. It wasn't really a surprise. After all, the thing was only designed to move someone around in a small laboratory — not to send them rocketing across the void.

Why this should have bothered me, when I had already decided things were hopeless I don't know.

But suddenly a blind rage swept over me. I ripped off the belt and was on the verge of throwing it away out of pure disgust, when the germ of an idea stopped me.

"How do these things recharge?" I wondered.

I turned the thing over and found the valve where the air source plugged in. My heart leapt at the sight of the familiar configuration. Uncertain, hardly daring to hope, I took a deep breath — and disconnected the hose from the cannisters strapped on my back.

They were a perfect match — which meant I could attach the airtanks to the belt and get the kind of power I had been missing before. The only problem, of course, was that I couldn't breathe whatever air I blew through the belt.

In other words, the faster I headed for home, the less time I would have to make it.

I barely hesitated. Shrugging myself out of the straps that held the air-pack, I maneuvered the cannisters around in front of me.

The whole process was pretty awkward, but I finally got the air hose connected to the belt.

I pressed the button that would start the air flowing.

For a second I was afraid it was going to be too much for the belt. The helmet on my space-suit had a feeder mechanism to diffuse the com-pressed oxygen and let it in slowly. The belt, less sophisticated, just let the gas through in a rush.

The results were pretty spectacular. I flew backward as though I had been shot out of the proverbial cannon.

I felt a surge of hope that I might make it home after all. Unfortunately, I also felt a strong urge to breathe again. Disconnecting the hose from the belt, I plugged it back into my helmet and took a few breaths. Then I filled my lungs as full as I could and reconnected the hose and the belt.

Since there was no friction and no gravity, none of the momentum I had gained the first time was lost. I could keep building speed this way as long as my air held out.

This breathe and accelerate pattern kept me busy for the next hour. Between switching the hose back and forth from the helmet to the belt and trying to make sure I kept myself on course, I barely had time to worry about how much trouble I was in.

At least until the second air tank ran out.

I switched to the third tank and tried to figure the odds. I was still a long way from home. But by now I was traveling considerably faster than I had been before. I began to think there was a slim chance I might actually make it back alive.

Of course once I got there, I would be faced with two more problems: one, I would have to slow myself down again; two, I would have to figure out some way to actually get back into the colony. (After all, I couldn't just float up to the air lock and ring the doorbell.)

I was still trying to figure out how to handle those things when I ran out of air altogether.

13. Elmo Explains

The first thing I saw when I opened my eyes was Cassie's face. She was looking down at me with what seemed like real concern.

The sight confused me for a minute. I thought maybe I had died and gone to heaven. I muttered something about angels and wings, then closed my eyes again.

"Rusty!" said a sharp voice. "Wake up."

It was Dr. Chang.

I opened my eyes again. I was still feeling pretty groggy, but this time I managed to get a look around me.

I was in a medium-sized space vehicle, one of the ones usually used to carry materials back and forth between the colony and some of the manufacturing modules. Cassie and Dr. Chang were kneeling beside me, Dr. Chang holding my wrist between her slim fingers. Both of them looked relieved to see me open my eyes again.

"What are a couple of nice girls like you doing in a place like this?" I asked. All right, I'll grant it was a pretty feeble joke. But feeble is a pretty good description of how I was feeling right then.

"We were out looking for space litter," said Cassie, "and we found you." Her words were barbed, but her voice was soft, and I could tell she was worried about me. For a minute I considered fainting again, just to see how much I could milk the situation.

Helen nipped that idea in the bud by chiming in with the real explanation of what had happened — or at least part of it. "Elmo sent us," she said. "I'd tell you all about it, but he prefers to explain how brilliant he is in person."

I nodded and closed my eyes. Cassie put her hand on my forehead. "He must be exhausted," she said. "I would be, if I'd been through something like this."

I bit down on the smile nibbling at the corners of my mouth and kept my eyes closed. Cassie left her hand on my forehead.

Dr. Puckett floated behind his desk, looking as smug as a cat who's just swallowed a canary.

"OK," I said. "The suspense is killing me. Tell me how you found me."

The big man smiled contentedly. "Well, I keep a watch on the colony's monitoring systems," he said. "Partly because I don't trust the jamokes who run the place, mostly because I just like keeping an eye on my baby. Anyway, to help me keep in touch, I've programmed my computer to alert me when the scanners pick up anything unusual heading in our direction. You, my free-floating young friend, fell into that category. You're lucky you did, since without your scooter, you were too small for the traffic control guys to pay any attention to you. And since you weren't on a path that would bring you into a direct collision with us, you didn't kick off the alarms in the monitoring station either. So of course those morons just ignored you.

"Fortunately, my own system considered you an interesting anomaly. Once I was alerted, it didn't take long for me to realize that this mystery object was accelerating in a very unusual fashion.

"Naturally, that made me curious. No natural object that I'm aware of could have such an erratic pattern of movement. Yet this thing was too small for any kind of spacecraft we use. A tantalizing mystery indeed.

"I decided that since you have access to a scooter, I would ask you to zip over and take a look at this strange object — not yet realizing that it and you were one and the same!

"But when I couldn't locate you, I started putting two and two together. It seemed to me that if you really are on to some kind of crime here, it was not too far-fetched to imagine someone might like to send you on a one-way trip to nowhere. It was only a brilliant guess, of course. But if it was accurate, it was urgent. I rushed the girls out to do a check on my mysterious object and sure enough — there you were."

"I guess I owe you my life," I said.

"Yes," said Dr. Puckett. "You do. But don't

worry. I'll find some way for you to pay me back."

"Boy, are you in trouble," said Helen.

"Well, now that you understand how you got out of that mess, why don't you tell us how you got into it," said Dr. Puckett.

Since I was dying to talk about what had happened to me, I didn't need any more encouragement. I launched into my story and was gratified when it was greeted with expressions of horror in all the appropriate places.

When I was finished, Dr. Puckett did something I'll never forget.

He came out from behind his desk and gave me a hug.

"You," he said, "are one terrific kid. Your grandfather should be very proud."

I have a hard time handling compliments. In fact, sometimes I think it would be easier to get yelled at than to have someone say something nice to me. Anyway, I was really touched. But I didn't know what to say.

The silence was about to get uncomfortable, when Helen spoke up. "Well, I might as well go right ahead and die," she said. "Because I don't think there's anything left that can surprise me."

"Give me five minutes," said Dr. Puckett, returning to his desk. "I'll think of something that'll knock your socks off."

"I'll take a rain check," said Helen. "If you can stop being cute for a while, maybe we can decide what to do about the new information Rusty has turned up."

"Let's start with something simple," said Dr. Puckett. "Like a computer check on Mr. Henry Smollin."

He tapped a few commands into the keyboard at his desk.

"Here he is," he said. He tapped a few more keys, and the wall behind him displayed a photograph.

"That's him!" I cried. "That's the guy I saw in the waste tank."

"Interesting," said Dr. Puckett. "The computer has him listed as alive and well." He punched a few more numbers into his console.

"What are you doing now?" asked Cassie.

"Giving Mr. Smollin a call," said Dr. Puckett.

He propped up the phone screen on his desk, adjusting the angle so Helen, Cassie, and I could see it without being seen ourselves.

I started to say something, but the vid-phone was already ringing. I still might have tried to cut it off, just so I could have a minute to think about this before I had to deal with it.

But the screen on Dr. Puckett's desk lit up after the second ring.

"Can I help you?" asked a deep, friendly sounding voice.

"It's him," I whispered. "It's the guy I saw in the waste tank!"

"You mean the one who's supposed to be dead?" hissed Cassie.

I nodded, staring at the screen with my mouth open and trying to decide whether or not I had finally and completely lost my mind.

14. Conference

"The living shall die, the dead shall live, and music will untune the skies," said Dr. Puckett.

"Care to run that by us again?" said Helen. "I think I had a potato in my ear the first time."

"I was just quoting an old poem," said Dr. Puckett. "It seemed appropriate."

The four of us were floating in a ring around Dr. Puckett's desk, trying to make some kind of sense out of what had just happened.

The vid-phone was off. After he heard me tell Cassie that Smollin was indeed my "dead" man, Dr. Puckett had severed the connection with a hasty "Sorry, wrong number."

As he explained it later, while he was not exactly at a loss for words (I doubt that will *ever* happen) he didn't think it would be a good idea to ask Smollin if he was indeed the man who had been spotted swimming in the waste recycling tank two days ago. "He might have found the question offensive," said Dr. Puckett primly. Helen pointed out that, to her knowledge, this was the first time the possibility of offending someone had ever stopped Dr. Puckett from saying anything that floated into his head.

Dr. Puckett chose to ignore the comment.

"So what do we do now?" asked Cassie.

"Organize our thoughts a bit," said Dr. Puckett, punching a few buttons on his desk. Once again the wall behind him went dark. His fingers flew over the keys. Suddenly a vertical line divided the wall from ceiling to floor. Amber letters about a foot and a half high centered themselves over each column. "WHAT WE KNOW," said the left side of the wall. "WHAT WE DON'T KNOW," said the right.

"Your input is invited," said Dr. Puckett.

I kept quiet for the time being, since about the only thing I could say with any certainty at the moment was "I'm confused," and I didn't think that was what Dr. Puckett was looking for.

"The 'DON'T KNOW' side is a lot easier," said Helen. "We don't know who — or what — Rusty really saw in the waste tank. We don't know who put it there. We don't know why they put it there. And we don't know who tried to kill Rusty a few hours ago."

"Not bad for starters," said Dr. Puckett, tapping away at the keys on his desktop. "But as we can see, some of that leads us to things we do know, or at least can be pretty sure of. For example, only a day ago the opening question on the left side would have been 'Is there really anything strange going on around here?' — or, more rudely phrased, 'Is Rusty losing his marbles?' But with the attempt on Rusty's life, it seems safe to assume that there is indeed some funny business going on."

"And it must be centered in the BS Factory," I said, breaking my vow of silence in a record forty-five seconds.

"Agreed," said Dr. Puckett, adding that to his list. "Which is why we have to do some additional investigation of the place. You are the logical candidate for that mission."

"But someone is trying to kill me!" I yelped.

"I thought you might mention that," said Dr. Puckett calmly. "You have to remember that they're trying to do it in a very accidental-looking kind of way. It's not like you're going to have people taking pot shots at you from behind the doorways. Whoever is involved in this doesn't just want to hide what they're doing. They want to hide the fact that there's anything going on at all. So they're not going to do something like blow your brains out in the hallway, since that will bring them unnecessary attention. However, I would suggest that you don't eat or drink anything while you're over there. And we'd better get a report filed on that scooter as soon as possible."

"I think I missed a step there," said Cassie. "What does filing a report on the scooter, which we should have done by now anyway, have to do with their fear of unnecessary attention?"

"It will help protect the two of you," said Puckett.

"The *two* of us?" asked Cassie, in a strangled kind of voice.

Dr. Puckett nodded. "You're going back to the

BS Factory with Rusty tomorrow. He'll tell them — oh, I don't know. Tell them she's your girlfriend, Rusty, and that you brought her over to show her around."

Cassie started to protest. "His girlfriend! Now look, Elmo . . ."

Puckett waggled a finger at her. "It's not going to hurt your reputation, my dear. The lad is not entirely ugly, you know. And showing off for his 'girlfriend' gives Rusty a reason that is understandable, if not valid, for poking around where he doesn't belong. Besides, I have several other purposes that will be filled by sending you over together. For one thing, except in the case of someone as astute as myself, two pairs of eyes are always better than one. Furthermore, one of you can stand guard while the other digs around in places where he or she doesn't belong. But your most important job, Cassie, will be to act as a kind of insurance policy for Rusty."

Cassie looked puzzled. So did I.

"It should be obvious," said Dr. Puckett. "Even if the thought of killing off an innocent bystander doesn't slow our villain down, the thought of the attention *two* deaths would bring to the BS Factory surely will. Which, to go back to your original question, is why we have to not only report the scooter incident, but report it in the right way."

"I've got it," I said. "Once we've reported it, whoever rigged the thing won't dare try it again. One failure like that could be an accident. If it happens twice, everyone will *know* something is going on."

Dr. Puckett nodded serenely. "You're coming along, young man. We might make a thinker out of you yet. What you didn't mention is that we have to make the report read as though *we* think it was an accident. That will keep the officials out of this. But it should also confuse our opponents a little, which is a useful tactic."

"I don't like it, Elmo," said Helen. "You're asking them to take too many risks. We'd better just turn this thing over to the authorities."

Dr. Puckett actually managed to look stern. "What authorities? The colonial management? This job calls for intellect, Helen. Intellect, logic, and deductive reasoning. Even two out of three wouldn't be bad on most days. But you know as well as I do that if you could combine the best three bureaucrats in this place you'd still be lucky to end up with more than one and a half of those traits."

I glanced at Cassie to see how she was taking this attack on her father's profession. Not well. Her eyes were smoldering, and I had a feeling she was about to make some angry response.

Dr. Chang beat her to the punch. "Elmo, I can put up with your oversized ego when it's only feelings that are getting hurt. But this time you're playing with people's lives."

"Not me," said Dr. Puckett. "But someone is. And that's exactly why we're keeping this to ourselves. We don't know what kind of person we're dealing with yet. About all we do know is that this person has a very small regard for human life. How small? That's the question, Helen. *How small*? One person, we don't even know who, is dead already. But for a combination of luck and intellect Rusty would be in the same condition. Where does a person who would commit two murders stop? How desperate is he? Desperate enough to kill again? To kill a dozen people? To kill a hundred? This colony is very well designed. But it is not sabotage proof, and it certainly isn't maniac proof. And until I know what we're dealing with, I'm not going to pass the situation on to some fuzzy-brained, fumble-fingered administrative assistant who just might push our mysterious friend into doing something we'll all regret should we live long enough to see it."

Well, as you know, I already took this thing pretty seriously. But by the time Dr. Puckett finished that little speech, I was wondering if maybe I should just bow out. I get pretty fuzzy-brained and fumble-fingered myself sometimes. I didn't want to be the one to make a mistake that pushed our murderer over the deep end.

I said so.

"Too late, Rusty," said Dr. Puckett. "You're already in this up to your eyebrows. Besides, if *you* do something stupid you'll at least have the brains to let me try to fix it — a situation that does not, I assure you, apply when we are dealing with the bureaucracy of this place."

Helen Chang's dark eyes were flashing. "Elmo," she said, "if what you just said has any validity, I may see it after I get finished sorting through all the nonsense you wrapped it in. But unless you need me for anything else right now, I've got some work of my own to finish."

Dr. Puckett nodded, like a statue of the Buddha coming momentarily to life, and Helen left the room. He rolled his eyes as she left, then twitched his head toward Cassie. Without a word, she moved to follow Helen.

"She'll calm down in a little while," he said when we were alone. "This sometimes happens when I overestimate her tolerance for my ego. None of which changes the reality of the problems I just enumerated."

"So what do we do now?" I asked.

"Two things. First we file a report on the scooter incident. Then I'm going to show you something that should give you a clue about what's going on over there."

"You mean you know?" I asked in surprise.

"Well, I don't know exactly who did what to whom," he said. "But I do have a pretty good idea of what it's all about." He sighed. "I suppose Helen will be angry with me over that, too. You see, I *was* being a little overdramatic when I made my big speech. Not that the danger isn't real, mind you. It is. But I do doubt that anyone has actually been killed yet."

He paused, then looked me in the eye. "The trick is to see if we can keep it that way."

15. Bootleg Research

"You're going to like this," said Dr. Puckett, pushing a button and settling back into a chair.

It was the first time I had actually seen him sit in a chair. But then, it was the first time I had ever seen an easy chair in an elevator — if, indeed, that's what this thing actually was. It had the general feel of an elevator. But it was far more luxurious than any elevator I had ever seen before.

The door closed and we started to move. At least I had been right about that much. It *was* an elevator.

We had reached the elevator by way of Dr. Puckett's luxurious living quarters, which were by far the largest I had seen in the colony.

The elevator stopped. The door slid open, and we stepped out into a small room. There was gravity here, but it was very low, maybe a tenth of normal. Since his functional weight here was only about 15 kilograms, Dr. Puckett was able to bound across the floor like a ballet dancer. When he reached the other side of the room he pushed a button, then watched, smiling, while part of one wall peeled away to provide a clear view of the stars beyond.

It was breathtaking.

Unfortunately, it was also a little too reminiscent of my recent adventure for me to appreciate it properly.

"What is this place?" I asked.

"One of my hobbies," said Dr. Puckett jovially. "A private observation port I worked into the plans when the colony was still in the dreaming stages."

I looked at him. "How do you get away with things like that?" I asked.

He chuckled. "Power generally comes from a combination of sources, Rusty. To begin with, I have a great deal of money. However, contrary to popular opinion, money is often not enough. Fortunately for me, I also control the patents on a number of concepts without which these colonies can't be built. That gives me quite a bit of clout when I want to negotiate for something special. But what really puts me over the edge when I want something like this is the fact that, when I choose to be, I am a genuinely likeable person." He smiled. "You may find that hard to believe. But it's true. I'm not talking about being a bootlicker; everyone despises that kind of person, no matter how much they might enjoy the flattery. It's just that underneath all the prickles, I'm a nice guy."

I thought about it for a moment. If someone had asked me to describe Dr. Puckett, I would have started out by saying he was the crankiest, most obnoxious human being I had ever met.

Yet why was I here now? Because my grandfather had asked Dr. Puckett to help me. At first I had thought Gramps was calling in a favor. But that wasn't the case. My grandfather knew Dr. Puckett because the scientist had helped him out with some stories. And now the man was helping me, too. Not because he owed Gramps a favor. Simply because he felt like it.

I realized something else about him. Because he had chosen to be larger than life himself, Elmo Puckett made life exciting for others. Being with him gave even the most routine moments a feeling that you were hovering at the edge of something special. I had only known Elmo for two days. But I knew if I survived this investigation, I would very much want to remain part of his inner circle. In fact, I would probably do just about anything he asked of me.

It was then that I began to understand how Dr. Puckett got away with so much. It wasn't his scorn people feared. It was the possibility of losing his presence in your life.

Dr. Puckett took his place at a console filled with dials, switches, and a variety of video monitors stretched across one side of the room. "Sit here," he said, motioning beside him.

I sat.

"This is what I really wanted to show you," he said. The excitement in his voice was contagious. "Take a look out there."

He pointed toward the lower right corner of

the window. I stared, wondering what I was supposed to be looking for.

"See that bright spot — about half a meter up and maybe ten centimeters in?"

I nodded.

"OK, watch the monitor in front of you. I'll give you a close-up view."

He fiddled with the console a bit and suddenly a familiar looking object appeared on the screen. It was one of the colony's radio-telescopes, a complicated construction of tubes and flat surfaces larger than the colony itself. There were a dozen of these telescopes in all, stationed in an enormous ring around the colony.

"Let's see what it's focused on," said Dr. Puckett. He tapped away at the console. The wall slid back into place. I heard a clicking noise, and then a picture of a reddish disk appeared on the blank surface.

"Mars," said Dr. Puckett. "Dr. Yolen is monitoring the weather conditions for the Morigi/Russell exploration party."

I stared at the wall in fascination. Good pictures of Mars aren't that unusual, of course. But it was something else to see the planet as it was *at this moment.* I heard the keys clicking; the picture zoomed in to show more details — first a red desert scattered with enormous boulders, then Olympus Mons, the famous giant volcano that stands more than two and a half times as tall as Mount Everest.

Before I had begun to have enough of looking at the ancient planet, Dr. Puckett changed the picture again.

"Io," he said, as a slightly egg shaped object appeared on the wall. The Jovian moon was mottled with shades of yellow, orange, red, and brown. As Dr. Puckett continued to enlarge the image I saw a huge gaseous plume billowing up from the surface. One of the volatile satellite's volcanoes was in full eruption.

More clicking keys, and the picture changed abruptly yet again. This time the screen showed a luminous globe floating in a sea of darkness, its surface a shifting mixture of blues and whites.

"Home," said Dr. Puckett. The tone in his voice was unmistakably, if somewhat surprisingly, wistful. Not that it wasn't easy to be wistful for a place that, from this viewpoint at least, was really remarkably beautiful.

All this impressed me. But I couldn't figure out what it had to do with whatever was going on at the BS Factory.

"It's very pretty," I said cautiously.

"Pretty?" cried Dr. Puckett. "Calling that 'pretty' is like saying the universe is 'big.' You ain't lying, but you certainly ain't doing it justice. Anyway, I have something else I want to show you."

He tapped a few more keys. A chart appeared on the monitor in front of me. As near as I could make out, it was a list of the twelve radio-telescopes, along with information on what they were currently monitoring, who was using them, and what priority level was given to both the user and the project.

"We'll use number nine," said Dr. Puckett.

"Farnsworth isn't doing anything important with it right now, and that's where I have the biggest block of data built up."

"What are you doing?" I asked at last.

"Painting a picture of the universe," said Dr. Puckett.

"Well," I said somewhat sharply, "that explains everything."

Dr. Puckett laughed. "Hoisted by my own petard!" he exclaimed. "You'd better watch out, Rusty. I may be catching. Spend too much time with me and you, too, may develop a reputation for cranky superciliousness."

"Whatever that means," I said.

"Look it up," replied Dr. Puckett. (I did; it's a twenty dollar way of saying "snotty.")

"Can we get back to the universe?" I asked, trying to take the conversation someplace that would do me some good.

"Certainly," said Dr. Puckett jovially. "For the last year I've been using this radio-telescope to examine the ultraviolet radiation from a sector of space twenty billion light years away from here. Think about that for a minute, Rusty. The light I'm looking at is twenty billion years old. When I examine it — for example when I analyze a quasar in that area — I'm not seeing what that quasar looks like today. I don't have the slightest idea what it looks like today. For all I know it may not even exist any more. What I'm seeing is what it looked like *twenty billion years ago*. It's almost like having a time machine; I'm looking right into the past

— in this case back to the time when we think the universe was created."

He leaned back in his chair and stretched. "It's deliciously frustrating," he said. "Everytime we think we've made it back to the beginning, we find another layer to peel away. The well of the past is very deep indeed."

I still wasn't sure what this had to do with the BS Factory. But I was beginning to understand that when Dr. Puckett wanted to tell you something, he did it on his own schedule.

"That little project is pretty much smiled upon," he said, sitting up to the keyboard again. "I feed the data to a couple of scientists who are officially working on the topic, and nobody much minds.

"But I've got another little thing going here that really isn't approved." He wiggled his eyebrows and flashed me a wicked grin. "I'm searching for extraterrestrial intelligence."

That caught me by surprise. Because it was of such interest to my grandfather, I had been following the political conflict over that kind of research for the last couple of years. As far as I knew, it had been squashed on the grounds that it was a real money waster. That was a pretty good joke, considering the way the government was throwing money around on other things. My grandfather's opinion was that the underlying motive was fear of success; there was a powerful political/religious coalition that really didn't want to find anyone else out there — and certainly didn't want to do anything that would attract their attention.

"How are you getting away with that?" I asked.

Dr. Puckett put a finger beside his nose and gave me a conspiratorial wink. "I keep my mouth shut," he said. "At least, most of the time. There are people who know what I'm up to, of course. You can't keep a project this big, involving this much equipment, totally secret. But it's nothing unusual. There are a lot of scientists in ICE-3 working on projects that aren't officially approved. It's called bootleg research, and if you want my opinion, it's the most exciting stuff going on out here."

I wondered briefly if Dr. Puckett was conducting his search for alien intelligence because it interested him, or simply because he wasn't supposed to. I decided that wasn't fair. For all his outrageous behavior, he was a scientist right to the core. He couldn't be bothered with something that didn't interest him.

But I still wondered what he was trying to tell me. Surely not that the trouble in the BS Factory had something to do with aliens?

"So what's the clue?" I asked, as we were leaving the room a few minutes later.

Dr. Puckett rapped me on the head with his knuckles. "Good heavens, boy!" he cried. "When are you going to learn to think?"

And that was all the answer I could get out of him.

16. More Problems

My father is a physicist. My mother specializes in fusion techniques. We give new meaning to the phrase "nuclear family." This fact seems to carry over into our family arguments; generally speaking, the best way to measure them is in megatons.

I mention that now because we had a several megaton blowout that evening. It got started because my father had found out about the incident with the scooter, and he was angry.

Very angry.

"Why didn't you call one of us?" he shouted (over and over again). "One of us should have been notified."

"But I was all right," I kept saying. "Nothing really happened."

"Nothing happened?" cried my mother. "You were trapped in a scooter that's currently making a one-way trip out of the solar system. Then you were stranded, alone, in space for three hours. You ran out of air. You almost died. And you say '*nothing happened*'?"

"Well, I meant I was fine when it was all over," I said. "If there had been anything wrong with me, of course I would have gotten ahold of you. I just didn't want to bother you."

That was true. But it wasn't the whole story. The thing was, I had been so busy from the time I woke up in the rocket with Helen and Cassie to the time I left Dr. Puckett's observatory that contacting my parents had never crossed my mind. Even so, I still couldn't see what the fuss was all about. It's not like anything terrible had really happened. Just almost.

I think the real problem was the way my father heard about the incident. He has a friend in Traffic Control, and after Dr. Puckett and I reported the mishap with the scooter, this guy decided to call Dad and fill him in on the details. Hearing the story from someone else, instead of me, was what really had him riled up.

In any case, I guess I probably said some things I shouldn't have. I *know* they said some things they shouldn't have.

Anyway, it got worse and worse, until finally I decided I had had enough of the whole stupid argument and went storming into my bedroom. I slammed the door (which is a relatively stupid thing to do, because it only makes other people madder) and sat down to call my grandfather.

That was when the really terrible thing happened.

I waited for my grandfather to appear. But all I got on the screen was my father's face, which was still dark with anger. "Forget it, Rusty," he said. "I'm not going to have you running to your grandfather for sympathy every time you think you're being mistreated. I've locked your line. You'll just have to do something else instead. Like some studying maybe."

He clicked off. I was left sitting there staring at a blank screen and thinking things about my father that it is, believe me, better not to think.

The worst thing was, I hadn't been calling Gramps just to complain about my parents, though I probably would have started out with that. I was calling him because I needed his help sorting out the things that had happened to me that day — including that strange scene where Dr. Puckett had given me a "clue" to what he thought was going on in the BS Factory.

In the end, I spent the evening making notes on everything that had happened. I wrote out a list of all the events and the times they had occurred. I went over it and over it, looking for connections, trying to make some kind of sense out of it all.

But by the time I finally fell asleep, I was still as mystified as ever.

The next morning we met in Dr. Puckett's office for a brief strategy session.

On the wall behind his desk he had created a list of the total staff of the BS Factory, from the seven senior scientists right through the custodial workers.

There were twenty-five names in all, including mine.

"We are about to make an assumption," said

Dr. Puckett. "The reasoning for it goes like this —"

He put his huge hands in front of him and began ticking off points on his tobacco-stained fingers.

"One: yesterday, someone at the BS Factory tried to kill Rusty.

"Two: the only reason we know of for someone to want to kill this fine young man is that he spent the day asking questions someone didn't want answered — questions about the body in the waste tank.

"Three: therefore, while it is not a dead certainty, it seems reasonable to assume that the two incidents are connected — which means that body did indeed come from the BS Factory.

"Four: that means we can eliminate the rest of our suspects and concentrate all our efforts in this one place. Which is why Rusty and Cassie are going to spend the day over there poking around."

He smiled wickedly. "But before you go, I want you to look through these dossiers I had printed out."

He slid several folders across his desk. I took them and whistled in astonishment. There were seven in all — a complete "Eyes Only" file on each of the Mad Scientists.

"I pulled them out of the main computer last night," said Dr. Puckett. He turned to Dr. Chang. "Helen, I want you to initiate a visit with Hank Smollin. See what you can find out from him."

Helen nodded.

Dr. Puckett then proceeded to astound us all with his next announcement: "As for myself, it's likely I will run into Rusty and Cassie, since I, too, am going to visit the BS Factory today."

"What are you talking about?" asked Helen. It was clear from the tone of her voice that she didn't like this idea at all.

"I've been feeling a little peaked lately," said Dr. Puckett piously. I just found out I need a complete checkup . . ."

". . . with your personal physician, Antoine Twining," said Helen, finishing his sentence for him. "I should have seen this one coming."

"Of course you should have," said Dr. Puckett smugly. "It makes perfect sense, don't you think?"

"Perfect," said Helen sardonically. "Your concern for your health is legendary. Why I remember the last time you granted an interview. The lead sentence in the story was your now famous proclamation that you are, and I quote, 'the most gleefully unfit person in the entire solar system.' "

"I've always liked that comment," said Dr. Puckett serenely. "It seemed to encapsulate my personality rather nicely."

"It certainly provides a sense of your ego," snapped Helen. "But given that, who do you think is going to believe you when you say you want a physical — much less one that you have to leave your office to get?"

"Why, no one," said Dr. Puckett, "that's the wonderful thing about this. It makes a perfect excuse for me to go over there. But at the same time there won't be any doubt in anyone's mind that I'm really there for some other reason. It should strike a little fear into our enemy's heart, which is usually a worthwhile thing to do. Besides, while I'm there I'll have a chance to do a little looking around on my own. No offense to Rusty and Cassie, but there's nothing like seeing it with your own eyes.

"And will you really get a physical?" asked Helen warily.

"I had a physical just six months ago," said Dr. Puckett.

Helen snorted. "Twining stopped by, drew a blood sample, and gave you a lecture on your eating habits. That does not constitute a physical in anyone's mind but yours, Elmo. I repeat my question: are you really going to get a physical?"

Dr. Puckett made an expression of distaste. "I suppose I'll have to," he said. "Just to keep up appearances."

I could sense Helen's disapproval fading away. I had come to realize that taking care of Dr. Puckett was one of her main jobs. She might never have a chance like this again, and she knew it.

"Get moving," said Dr. Puckett. "I'll meet you over there."

We moved.

Millicent Carter looked surprised to see me. "Rusty!" she cried. "The way the guys from Traffic Control talked, I didn't expect to see you around until sometime next week. I think you're smart to be out flying right away though. If you wait too long after an experience like that, you may never get started again."

I suppose that's probably true. I had had trouble getting started even today. In fact, if Cassie hadn't been with me, I might just have convinced myself to put the whole thing off till another day. But I wasn't about to admit in front of her that I was afraid to fly again. Besides, just having someone with me made it easier; one of the worst things about yesterday had been the aloneness of it all.

I started to say something, but Millie cut me off.

"Listen, kid," she said, taking me by the arm, "I'm sorry."

"Hey, Millie," I said, "it's not your fault. Something went wrong with the scooter. Keeping those things in running order isn't your job."

"Yeah, I know," she said. "But somehow I feel responsible anyway. I suppose it's the mother in me. Now — are you gonna introduce me to your lady friend, or do I have to do it myself?"

I performed the introductions, and Cassie and I headed into the BS Factory proper. Before we had gone twenty feet I heard someone call my name from behind.

It was Dr. Hulan, the oldest and probably the testiest member of the Mad Scientists' Club. He was drifting down the corridor, clutching a stack of papers that went from his navel to his chin. Once he had our attention, he suggested that we help him.

Actually, "suggest" is probably too polite a description for Dr. Hulan's approach. His exact words were "Rusty! Stop flapping your gums and make yourself useful."

I relieved him of part of the load. Cassie lifted another eight or nine inches of paper off the stack.

Dr. Hulan looked considerably relieved.

After we had deposited the papers in his office, I introduced Cassie and asked him to explain his work to her.

Have I told you Rusty McPhee's First Law of Scientific Discourse? It goes like this: no matter how cranky or withdrawn they may seem, asking scientists to explain their work is like firing the starting gun for a race; the words are barely out of your mouth before they're off and running. This can cause a real problem if their work is classified, in which case they are torn between two powerful but conflicting urges: the need to babble about what they're doing and the need to avoid having some government agency bust their chops. In those circumstances the poor creatures usually start several sentences they can't finish, move on to unconnected words, blush, begin to sweat, and finally suffer a functional breakdown.

I'm certain there are exceptions to this rule. Dr. Hulan was not one of them.

We got the complete tour, or nearly so.

It was mind boggling. I barely knew Dr. Hulan, and that was only because he occasionally came into our lab to argue with Dr. Twining. I had been totally unaware of what he was working on.

Nanotechnology is the name for it, and it's one of those things where if he ever gets it right, it's going to change the world. He says there are a lot of scientists working on it. I think that's a little scary.

Basically, he's designing ways to manufacture things at the molecular level. For example, he showed us a situation where he was *growing* copper wire. He said by fiddling with the receptor molecules, he could adjust the thickness and the density of the wire.

"This guy scares me," whispered Cassie once, when Dr. Hulan was a few steps ahead of us.

"He's no gruffer than Dr. Puckett," I said.

"You don't understand. What he's *doing* scares me. It's too weird for words."

I didn't say anything then — partly because Dr. Hulan turned back to say something to us, partly because I agreed with her.

I never did find out what Dr. Hulan was going to say then, because we were interrupted by a voice from the intercom.

"Charles!" it said. "Come quickly! I need you!"

It was Dr. Durkin. He sounded desperate.

Ignoring us, Dr. Hulan hurried out of the room.

We were close on his heels.

17. Dr. Collins

Dr. Durkin's lab was a shambles. Tables were overturned. Equipment was scattered across the floor. There was broken glass everywhere.

Dr. Durkin himself didn't look much better. His lab coat hung in tatters about his shoulders, and he was covered with blood from several deep cuts.

He was standing in the far corner of the lab. Facing him, crouched on a table and making angry noises, was Ron — the chimp that had been so sick yesterday.

"Thank God, you're here," said Dr. Durkin as Dr. Hulan came through the door. "You've got to help me subdue him."

Then he spotted Cassie and me. "Rusty! Get out of here! And get that girl out of here!"

The words were barely out of his mouth when Ron jumped.

It was horrible. The chimp I had been going to cuddle yesterday attacked Dr. Durkin like a whirlwind made of teeth and claws.

"Charles," cried Dr. Durkin, "help me!"

Dr. Hulan rushed forward. I was right beside him.

Durkin and the chimp were on the floor now. Durkin managed to get one foot against Ron's chest. He thrust out with his leg and sent the chimp flying against the wall. The animal slumped to the floor, momentarily stunned.

"Don't touch him!" commanded Dr. Durkin, struggling to get back onto his feet. "Get the gun. It's in my desk."

Suddenly Ron was back on him, snapping and clawing again.

"Rusty," snarled Dr. Hulan as he headed back toward Durkin's desk. "Get that girl out of here *now*!"

"Cassie," I said. "Get out of here."

"Not unless you do, too," she said.

"Don't be stupid!"

"Don't you be stupid! Come on!"

Muttering angrily, I grabbed her arm and hustled her out of the room. Behind us I could hear shouting and the sound of more equipment hitting the floor.

Suddenly everything went quiet.

I waited a second, then pushed the intercom button next to the door.

"Dr. Durkin?"

But it was Dr. Hulan who answered. "Everything is under control, Rusty, I've anesthetized the chimp. Dr. Durkin is all right. I will handle things here. Please take the young lady elsewhere for the time being."

"But . . ."

"Do as I say!" said Dr. Hulan sharply. "I don't have time to argue."

I stared at the floor for a minute, then turned to Cassie.

"Come on," I said. "I guess we'd better go."

"Are things always this exciting around here?" she asked as we made our way down the hallway.

"Not until this week," I said. Then I turned on her. "Why wouldn't you get out of there when I told you to?" I asked angrily.

"Dr. Durkin told us both to go," she snapped back.

"But they might have needed my help," I said.

"Oh really?" she asked. "And what was wrong with that chimp?"

"I don't know," I said. "I think he's sick."

"Right. Which I assume is why Durkin told Hulan to use the gun. You don't tackle an animal like that with your bare hands unless you want to get sick, too. You might have been able to come up with something dumber than just wading into that fight. Offhand, I can't think of what it would have been."

I hate it when you're having an argument and the other person hits you with a piece of irrefutable logic like that. Spurred on by my adrenalin, I had been on the verge of making the same stupid mistake I had almost made yesterday.

"Let's go see Dr. Collins," I said, by way of changing the subject.

"Fine," said Cassie.

We walked on a little way. "What does this one do for a living?" she asked after a moment. "Grow spare parts for body transplants?"

"That's Dr. Twining's area," I said, ignoring her sarcasm. "Dr. Collins is studying the effects of weightlessness on the reproductive system. She's one of the world's foremost experts on the subject."

"I bet there aren't a whole lot of them to begin with," said Cassie. "It isn't a big topic in most science courses."

I might have sparred with her a bit on the topic, but my mind was still occupied by the terrible thing that had happened in Dr. Durkin's lab. We moved on in silence.

Martha Collins was a short, good-natured woman with twinkling eyes and a thick head of curly brown hair. She greeted us with enthusiasm, which seemed to make Cassie kind of nervous. ("I thought maybe she wanted to use us for some kind of experiment," she told me later.)

After I introduced Cassie and explained that I was showing her around the BS Factory, Dr. Collins offered to give us a tour of her lab. That wasn't as exciting as it might sound, since her experiments were pretty much confined to fruit flies and white mice. I suppose her findings are important. But they are not, believe me, anything that is going to change your day to day life.

Toward the end of the tour we were playing with some baby mice while Dr. Collins explained the effects that weightlessness had had on the mother during her pregnancy. We had just put the babies back in their cage and started to move on to the next area Dr. Collins wanted to show us, when a door slid open on the right-hand wall just ahead of us. One of Dr. Collins' research assistants stepped through. I caught a glimpse of what appeared to be several cages as the door slid shut behind him.

The researcher seemed startled to see us. He shot a questioning glance at Dr. Collins.

"It's OK, Max," she said. "I'm just giving them a tour of the operation."

Max nodded and continued on his way.

"What's that room for?" asked Cassie, indicating the door Max had just come through.

"Nothing much," said Dr. Collins. "It's primarily a rest area. Come on, there's something I want to show you over here. Then I really have to get on to my own work. But I hope you'll bring Cassie back sometime, Rusty. It's always nice to have a chance to show off one's work."

"What do you think?" said Cassie.

"About what?" I asked.

"About Dr. Collins, Einstein! What did you think I wanted your opinion on? Navel lint?"

"Actually, that can be a rather deep subject," I said. "I have some rather profound thoughts on the topic."

"Probably just more of your fuzzy thinking. Save it for later, and tell me what you think of Dr. Collins."

"Well, I think she did a good job of making sure we only saw what she wanted us to."

"You got that impression, too, huh?"

"Yep. And did you notice how nervous Max looked when he stepped out in front of us? I don't know what they've got in that back room, but I'll bet you a bowl of rabbit stew it's more than a couple of easy chairs and a coffee pot. In fact, I thought I saw some cages back there. But I couldn't be sure. Did you get a look through the door at all?"

Cassie shook her head, which caused her honey-colored hair to whisk over her shoulders in a very distracting way. "Couldn't see a thing. Max was in the way."

"We'll put that on our list of things to check out if we decide to get really snoopy," I said. "In the meantime, I have to get myself over to Dr. Twining's lab. It's time for my shift to start."

"Shall I come along, or do you think I ought to go out poking around on my own?"

"Come on along," I said. "I'd at least like you to meet the guy. Once I start working you might as well head out and do a little investigating on your own. It'll be pretty boring for you to just sit there and watch."

"Were you serious when you were talking about Dr. Twining's work earlier?" she asked as we made our way down the corridor.

"What did I say?"

"You know — about him growing spare body parts."

She gave a little shudder.

I laughed. "Serious, but seriously exaggerating. Dr. Twining's real project is limb and organ regeneration in mammals. I suppose if he ever really beats it, then he could use the same tactics for growing spare parts. But the real idea is to figure out how people can regrow their own parts when something happens to them."

When we got to the lab we found Dr. Puckett already there, cheerfully insulting Dr. Twining. Puckett ignored us, and I got the impression that he didn't want Dr. Twining to know we were working together. I couldn't see the point in that, but he was the boss.

Dr. Twining glanced at his watch. "I am stunned into near silence, Rusty. It is only ten minutes past the time you're supposed to be here; I didn't expect to see you for at least another twenty. If I can attribute this new punctuality to the charming young lady standing beside you then perhaps you'd better introduce us."

I did, and then let Dr. Twining introduce Dr. Puckett as if we had never met him before. I could tell from the look on the old scoundrel's face that he was enjoying the charade.

"Dr. Puckett is a patient of mine," said Dr. Twining, "though certainly the most exasperating one I have ever had to deal with."

Dr. Puckett beamed.

"Stop smiling," said Dr. Twining severely. "Despite your aggravating ways I'd like to keep you alive for a while longer — not an easy task, considering the way you treat yourself. That blood pressure situation is like a time bomb waiting to go off."

Dr. Twining turned to me. "You might as

well start your work, Rusty. I have a few more things to discuss with Dr. Puckett. Then I'll see if I can help you with that problem you were having yesterday." He turned back to Dr. Puckett. "If you'll wait just a moment, Elmo, I'll get you something for that blood pressure."

Dr. Twining turned to the cabinet behind his desk; Dr. Puckett took advantage of the moment to pass me a note. I went to my work station and unfolded it.

Cassie peered over my shoulder as I read it.

Rusty:
I've got the whole thing figured out. If you're still in the dark by the time you're done here today, come and see me. I will be glad to dispense enlightenment — though I may require several hours of lab duty as penance for your obtuseness.

— E.P.

"You know," whispered Cassie, "I honestly believe he may be the most annoying man in the world."

"The universe," I said. "He'd be offended at the suggestion of anything less."

18. Disaster

I had been staring at the same slice of frog brain for several minutes without really seeing it. Finally I decided to adjust my microscope.

It didn't do any good. The problem wasn't in the equipment. It was my brain that was out of focus. I couldn't think about anything except the mysterious events of the last few days — and the fact that they seemed to be getting more mysterious by the hour.

I was alone in the lab. Dr. Puckett had returned to the colony. Cassie had wandered off, ostensibly out of boredom, but really to do as much snooping as she could manage while she waited for me. And Dr. Twining, after helping me a bit with what I was studying, had disappeared into his private office.

"Sorry frog," I said at last, putting away my materials. "I'd hate to think you died in vain. But the truth is, you and I are just not connecting today."

Crossing to the message board, I picked up

the light pen and left a note in large glowing letters:

Dr. T —
I hit another snag in my research — out wandering around while I try to figure it out.
                                        Rusty

That was absolutely true, of course, as long as I didn't specify which "research."

Now what?

I thought maybe I'd try to find Cassie and see if we could do some more investigating together. I'm not sure that two heads are really better than one, but they're certainly less lonely.

I realized that made a good excuse to get back into people's labs: "Excuse me, but I'm looking for my girlfriend. I have to get back to the colony now, and I can't find her. Is she in here?"

Where to begin? I had six labs to choose from, and each of them had something that could do with a little investigation.

I decided to start with Dr. Durkin's lab. It was unlikely I would find Cassie there, but I was anxious to know what had happened after the fight with Ron.

I pressed the button beside Dr. Durkin's door. No one answered.

I tried the door; the lab was unlocked.

I hesitated only a moment before deciding to go in.

Someone had made a minimal effort to clean

the place up: most of the furniture was upright again, and some of the debris had been swept into piles. But for the most part it was still a shambles.

I kicked aside some glass and walked toward the back of the lab. I couldn't see any sign of Ron. I wondered what had happened to the little chimp.

The basic floor plan is pretty much the same for all seven labs in the BS Factory. The main section is a large research room, where the head scientist, assistants, and interns like myself do most of their work. Floor tracking and modular wall designs make it possible for each scientist to divide his or her lab to suit their own taste or needs. This may mean creating small darkrooms, or clean-air facilities that can keep any foreign particles larger than a few micros from entering an area and contaminating an experiment. Each lab also has a washroom, a few cubicles where the underlings have some desk space, and a private office for the head scientist.

I poked my head into the washroom. The floor was stained with blood. A stack of bloody towels in the far corner served as further reminder of the grisly fight that had taken place here earlier this morning.

I looked in the cubicles. They were empty.

I crossed the lab and stood at the entrance to Dr. Durkin's private office. I hestitated for a moment, then knocked.

No answer.

I pressed the speaker button; "Dr. Durkin?" I called.

No answer.

Again I hesitated. I guess I just wasn't born to be a snoop. The idea of stepping uninvited into someone's private office was really bothering me.

I reminded myself of the body in the waste tank, telling myself there was something dreadfully wrong around here, and I had to get to the bottom of it.

That was the noble excuse for investigating Dr. Durkin's office.

If I am really honest with myself, I have to admit that there was another reason. I was desperate to figure out what was going on before I had to go back to the colony that afternoon. I didn't think I would be able to face Dr. Puckett if I hadn't figured things out by then.

I came up with a compromise: if the door was unlocked, I would investigate; if it was locked, I would leave it alone and not try to break in.

It was unlocked.

"Dr. Durkin?" I called again as I stepped through.

No answer.

I looked around. I was standing in a medium-sized room. To my right was a large desk, littered with papers. On the wall behind it hung several framed photographs and documents.

There were two more doors in the room. One led to a private bathroom. The other was locked.

In the center of the room, resting on a metal table, was a large red box. It was made of thick plastic. The sides were red. The top was clear. A thick strip of some kind of caulking had been used to seal the top to the sides, so that the box was airtight.

Inside, looking peaceful and quiet, was Ron the chimp.

I could feel tears start to well up in my eyes. It didn't seem fair. He was such a sweet little guy. And then this had to happen.

I just didn't get it.

A sudden noise jolted me out of my mood. (It's funny how quickly fear can replace sorrow.)

It was the door on the far side of the room, the one that had been locked, sliding open.

I ducked down behind the table and held my breath. I really didn't want to be caught here.

The position made my bad hip uncomfortable. I wanted to move, but I didn't dare.

I heard the light, brushing steps that characterize someone walking in low gravity like this and the sound of the door sliding back into place. An odor of antiseptic, heavy and clinging, caused me to wrinkle my nose.

The footsteps crossed the room and stopped at the desk. I held my breath, hoping that was where they would stay.

After a few moments my curiosity got the better of me, and I peered around the lower corner of the table. (Another thing I learned from MacDonald of Terra: when you're trying to spy on someone, keep your head low.)

It was Dr. Durkin. He was half covered with

bandages (the parts of him that were still sticking out didn't look that good, either). He stood at his desk, flipping through a sheaf of papers. He had a strange expression on his face. It took me a while to figure it out (the bandages didn't help any). At first I thought it was anger. Then I decided it was desperation. Finally I realized what I was really seeing on his face. It was fear.

It soon became clear that Durkin couldn't find whatever it was he was looking for. After a moment he threw the papers into a drawer. He sat down at his desk and tapped a few keys on his keyboard. The printer started to whir. Several fresh sheets of paper shot out of a slot in the wall and landed in the basket on the upper corner of his desk. Dr. Durkin snatched them up, gave them a quick glance, and hurried out of the room.

The door slid shut. I waited a minute or two, to be sure he wasn't going to come right back in, then stood up. I almost fell back down; my hip was letting me know it didn't appreciate the abuse I had just given it.

I limped over to Durkin's desk and slid into his chair. The drawer where he had tossed the papers was locked. I checked the keyboard. It was still on.

That meant the password was already logged in.

I typed three keys — the "repeat previous operation" command.

The computer obliged by spitting out another stack of papers.

Feeling incredibly smug, I snatched the papers, stuffed them into my tunic, and got my butt out of there.

I hadn't gone far when I ran into Cassie.

"Rusty!" she said. "Thank goodness. I've been looking for you. We've got to get back to the colony as quickly as possible."

I didn't like the tone in her voice.

"Is something wrong?" I asked.

She nodded her head. Suddenly I saw that there were tears in her eyes.

"It's Elmo," she said.

Whatever it was, she was having trouble getting it out.

"Cassie," I said, "what is it? What's going on?"

She took a deep breath; the words came out in a kind of a sob.

"I think he's dead."

19. The Interview

The trip back to the colony was pretty grim. Cassie stared straight ahead without saying a word. I concentrated on piloting the scooter and let the silence hang heavy and unbroken between us.

What *had* happened, as near as we could make out, was that the exertion involved in leaving his lair and traveling to the BS Factory had been too much for Elmo Puckett's overworked heart. Two hours after he returned to ICE-3, Helen Chang found him slumped across his desk.

She called for medical assistance, of course. And then she had put in a call to Dr. Twining.

Which was how the information had gotten to us; shortly after Helen's message came in, Cassie had wandered back into Dr. Twining's lab looking for me. She saw at once that he was terribly disturbed, so she asked him what was wrong. He had filled her in on the situation while preparing a large piece of medical equipment he needed to take back to the colony with him.

His scooter was just ahead of us now; we had run into him again at the docking area, where he was trying to wrestle that piece of equipment, which turned out to be a treatment table designed for low-gravity use, into his ship.

"Rusty, give me a hand with this," he said gruffly. "If I can get it over to the colony quickly enough, I may be able to save a man's life."

The problem wasn't that the table was heavy, of course: in the reduced gravity of the BS Factory it weighed next to nothing. It was just that it was so big: a box-shaped thing at least two meters long and a meter square at the ends.

When we finally got it into his scooter, Millie cleared him for take-off almost instantly.

It had been a strange scene. As of yet, Dr. Twining wasn't aware of our connection to Dr. Puckett. As far as he was concerned, I was just helping him with an urgent task; he had no idea that it probably seemed even more urgent to Cassie and me than it did to him.

Well, he would find out soon enough. I hoped he wouldn't be too mad about the deception. But it had been Dr. Puckett's idea to begin with — and the loading area really hadn't seemed like the right place to set him straight.

"Do you think he has a chance?" asked Cassie, as we followed Dr. Twining's ship into the landing area.

I didn't know what to say. I wanted to be warm and comforting, to say "Don't worry, it'll be all right, I'm sure he's gonna make it." But that was a lot of garbage, and I knew it. The thing was, I couldn't bring myself to say the truth either, which was that the odds were Dr. Puckett was gone already. It didn't make any difference. Inside we both knew it.

Dr. Twining didn't wait for us at the spindle, of course. He moved on to Dr. Puckett's office as quickly as possible. I imagine the emergency system had already commandeered an elevator for him, making it possible for him to move almost directly from his ship to the Hub.

It took Cassie and me a little longer. When we finally got to the office, Dr. Chang was waiting in the book-lined foyer where I had first met her, just three days before.

"Dr. Twining is with him now," she said grimly. "He asked me to leave the room."

She seemed offended.

I felt bad for her. Even so, I thought Dr. Twining was probably smart to have sent her out.

Here's why: before he began his career in research, Antoine Twining had spent several years as a practicing physician in a college community. When he started there, he had made the naive assumption that letting scientifically trained people observe a treatment situation would not be a problem.

"It didn't take me long to learn that professional behavior frequently flies out the window when someone you care about is dying," he told me one afternoon, when we were talking about his past experiences. "The last straw came on the day I was trying to start a woman's heart with shock treatment." He paused, as if he was remembering the scene. "She was convulsing, naturally, and her imbecile of a husband — who had a doctorate in biology, mind you! — this *imbecile* flung himself across her body crying 'You're killing her! You're killing her!' Well, that was the third time I almost lost a patient because I was distracted by husband, wife, or whatever, and I vowed never to let them stay in the room with me again."

Cassie started to speak when we heard some thumping from beyond the doorway. My imagination painted a picture of what was going on in there.

It wasn't pretty.

Personally, I was just as glad to be out here.

The noise stopped. "Are the other medics in there?" Cassie asked.

Helen shook her head. "They had already given up by the time Dr. Twining got here," she said. Her voice was trembling, but she kept herself under control.

More thumping, and then the door opened.

Dr. Twining came out, shaking his head. "I'm sorry," he said.

Cassie began to wail.

Dr. Puckett's body was strapped to the treatment table Dr. Twining had brought with him from the BS Factory. The table itself was held to the floor by electromagnetic devices in its base. I assumed this was one of the reasons he had brought the thing with him; it can't be easy to work on a heart patient in zero-gravity.

Dr. Twining had closed Dr. Puckett's eyes and folded his hands over his chest.

I floated near the table, looking down at my friend. I had only known the man for three days, but I felt like something had been ripped out of the inside of me.

Helen and Cassie floated nearby. Dr. Twining waited quietly near the door. He was going to take the body with him when he left, so that it could be prepared for final services.

I knew from the look on his face when he came back into the foyer that he had been surprised to find Cassie and myself there. But it clearly wasn't the right time for questions. I imagined that I would have some heavy-duty explaining to do later.

That really didn't make any difference right now. My attention was focused on the corpse strapped to the table.

It didn't look like Elmo Puckett anymore, of course. Puckett the man had been too filled with life for an uninhabited body to ever truly look like him.

Still, it was his shape and form, or nearly so, and it hurt to look at it. I say "nearly so" because the twin distresses of heart attack and convulsive therapy had left their marks.

Even so, I stared at the body as if I was trying to burn it into my brain — as if somehow that would help me keep him as part of me.

It was like looking at a volcano that had gone

suddenly dormant. I kept expecting the body to open its eyes and make some insulting remark about people who were too stupid to know when a man was just taking a nap.

But it didn't.

And it wasn't going to.

Maybe if we hadn't been so upset, it would have been easier for us to see the most important thing about the body. In my own defense, I want to say that it's hard to think clearly when you feel like there's a five hundred pound rock sitting on your chest.

Even so, for the amount of time I spent looking at that mountainous body, that round face, those smooth, pink hands folded over his chest, I should have put things together sooner.

After a while Dr. Twining cleared his throat — a little signal that we had had enough time, and he wanted to be about his business.

We moved away from the body. He touched a switch on the table and turned off the electromagnets. He was able to lift the table with one hand, but he asked me to help him guide it through the door.

"I want to talk to you later," he said as we moved through the foyer. His voice was soft, but very intense. I wasn't sure if he was angry or just curious.

Two paramedics waited outside the door to help with the table.

I moved back inside to be with Helen and Cassie.

The rest of the day passed in kind of a blur. I remember Helen telling us that she had talked to Hank Smollin, but that he hadn't been much help. He had been fired from the BS Factory six months ago and really didn't know what might be going on over there now. He did mention that while at first he couldn't figure out why he had been fired, he later decided it was for asking too many questions. He thought there might be something funny going on over there.

This did not qualify as big news.

Finally, reluctantly, the three of us separated to go to our own homes.

Things were relatively quiet at the apartment. My parents gave most of the dinner table conversation over to Elmo's death, which was the biggest thing to happen in the colony for some time. I pretty much kept my mouth shut. They didn't know I had been working with the man, and I didn't think this was the time to tell them. In fact, I just didn't feel like talking.

I tried to call my grandfather (my father had unlocked my line again) but he was off at a writers' conference; all I got was a recording of his smiling face, telling anyone who called to try again in a few days.

I remembered the papers I had duplicated in Pieter Durkin's office, which I had been carrying with me ever since. I spread them out on my desk. They were filled with complicated formulas and drawings of several related cell forms. Something about them bothered me. But even with my background in biochemistry, I couldn't make any real sense of them. I needed some background information before I could connect them to anything.

Frustrated, I turned on the evening broadcasts, which were full of information about Elmo's life and work. They showed (several times) an interview he had granted just a year ago. As usual, he had refused to be photographed. But the clip did include several segments shot over his shoulder, his voice explaining what he was doing as his hands tapped out equations on his trusty computer.

Basically, it was stuff I knew. After all, the man had been a "living legend." The media had been doing articles and features about him for years. I watched it anyway. If nothing else, I knew Dr. Puckett would enjoy the fuss he had created by passing away.

But something about the interview kept nagging me. Finally I taped it, then ran it several more times for myself.

His hands. What was it about his hands?

It wasn't until I was trying to go to sleep that everything finally clicked into place.

When it hit me I stood up so fast I knocked over my chair. Then I gave myself one of those clichéd slaps on the forehead.

But I figured I deserved a solid whack.

I couldn't believe what a dunce I had been.

20. Midnight Excursion

"Cassie? It's Rusty."

"Rusty! Are you crazy? It's almost eleven o'clock."

"I know. I'm glad you answered. I was afraid I might get your father."

She frowned at me. "What do you want?" she asked.

I took a deep breath. "Can you get free later tonight, after everyone is asleep? I want to go back to the BS Factory."

"You are crazy!" she said; I could see her reaching forward to snap off the screen.

"Cassie, wait!"

She hesitated.

"Listen, I don't want to talk about it right now. But we need to do a little more snooping around over there, when there's not so many people around. I'm going anyway. But I thought you might want to come along."

"Why don't you ask Helen?" she said.

It was a reasonable question. In fact, I had tried to ask Helen — mostly because I thought she might take me more seriously than I expected Cassie to.

Unfortunately, Helen was in no condition to take anyone seriously, much less go out on a possibly dangerous investigation. Of the three of us, she had been hardest hit by Dr. Puckett's death, and she was still in a state of intense grief. It had taken a long time for her to answer when I called, and when she did come on the line her eyes were red and puffy from weeping. What bothered me more was that her voice was slurred and drowsy, and she seemed to have trouble focusing on what I was saying. I was beginning to suspect foul play when she apologized for her condition and explained that her doctor had given her a sedative because of her emotional state. Feeling terrible for having intruded on her private grief, I made up a little story about having called to see how she was doing and rang off as quickly as possible.

Cassie didn't need to know all that right now. "She's not available," I said simply.

Cassie sighed. She looked over her shoulder. "All right," she said. "What time?"

"Can you meet me at the elevators at two o'clock?"

"Two o'clock? You're out of your mind!"

I didn't feel like arguing. "I know that. Are you in, or not?"

She hesitated. "Oh, all right. I'm in. I suppose working with Elmo damaged my brain. But I know he'd be disappointed in me if I didn't come."

Then her eyes started to fill up, and she clicked off.

I lay down on my bed and tried to think.

She was waiting when I got there.

"You're late!" she hissed.

Of course I was late. I'm always late. It's the stupidest thing about me. But I didn't want her to know that.

"I had a hard time getting out of the apartment," I hissed. Which was true. I had stumbled noisily over a footstool, almost awakened my parents, and given my bum hip a major twist that was still throbbing.

We took the elevator in to the Hub and then another out the spindle to the area where the scooters were docked. I inserted my I.D. card into the mechanical guard and punched in my personal code number.

The small screen on the front of the guard lit up.

"PERMISSION DENIED"

Muttering angrily, I punched in a code requesting to know why.

A copy of my personal I.D. form appeared on the screen. It held a lot more information than I needed to know and certainly more than I cared to have Cassie know, including my height, my weight, and my middle name. (All right — it's Cuchulain, a fact which can be blamed entirely on my Irish grandfather, and the one thing for which I have never forgiven him. Are you satisfied now?) Highlighted at the

bottom of the grid was the pertinent information. "Level One Access."

I touched those words, which was a request
for more information. The display disappeared
and a new screen came up, explaining exactly
what "Level One Access" allowed.

It didn't allow much. And one of the things it
didn't allow was signing out a scooter in the
middle of what passed for night in ICE-3.

I pushed a button and retrieved my card.

"Let me try," said Cassie.

She slipped her own card into the machine.
A few second later we were on our way to a
scooter.

"The long arm of Dr. Elmo Puckett," she said
hoarsely as we walked past the guard. "If you
had continued to work with him, you'd have
high level access, too. I was never sure if he
got it for me because he believed in being prepared for emergencies, or simply because he
knew I wasn't supposed to have it, and it tickled
his fancy to provide it. I can't even pilot one of
these things. My father didn't want me to learn
yet."

I know it was completely petty of me, but I
was glad that at least I would be doing the
driving.

I was also glad Cassie didn't take advantage
of the situation to make a few remarks about
how far I would have gotten if she hadn't come
along. Maybe she was starting to mellow a
little.

We docked at the BS Factory without incident. To my astonishment, Millicent Carter was on duty.

"Millie!" I said, when we climbed out of the scooter. "What are you doing here?"

"I might ask you the same thing," she said.

Cassie jumped right in. "I asked him to bring me over," she said, smooth as silk. "I have an important assignment due first thing in the morning. I was up late working on it when I realized I left some of my most important documents here this afternoon." She moved her hands in a small gesture of helplessness that was totally unlike her and also totally effective. "All the confusion, you know. . . . Anyway, I *have* to have it first thing in the morning, or I'm in real trouble. But I don't even have a license. So I asked Rusty to bring me over." She looked at me adoringly. "I think it was awful nice of him to bring me over at this time of the night. He hardly complained at all."

She was so good I almost believed that line of baloney myself!

Millie seemed satisfied. "It must be the night for wake-up calls," she said to me. "I got a buzz from the monitoring system that there was some kind of malfunction in the automatic docking mechanism." She looked thoughtful for a moment. "Come to think of it, it's a good thing I got here ahead of you. You might have been in real trouble if I hadn't."

Just what we needed: more trouble!

"Well, go ahead and get your stuff," said Millie. "I'll be busy here for quite a while yet."

"You're a pal, Millie," I said.

"Yeah, I know. Me and the rest of the dogs. Man's best friends. Scram before I hit you with a wrench."

We scrammed.

"You were brilliant," I said to Cassie, once we were out of earshot.

She shrugged. "I had to be. You think that woman is the salt of the earth. I'm not willing to trust *anyone* in this place until we figure out what's going on."

I decided to drop the subject.

"So where do we go now, Sherlock?" she asked.

"Let's start with Dr. Twining's lab."

"Haven't you had enough time there?" she asked.

"Not quite," I said, leading the way down the hall. "A year wouldn't be enough, if I wasn't looking for the right thing. Ten minutes should do it, now."

"Aren't we mysterious?" said Cassie.

I didn't say anything. If I were wrong, I was going to look awfully stupid. Since I was tired of looking stupid, I thought I'd just wait and see where I really stood before I said anything this time.

So instead of opening my mouth, I opened the door to the lab.

Then I opened my mouth.

Actually, it opened itself as my jaw headed for my knees.

I had expected the place to be deserted. Instead, I found myself face to face with a very agitated Dr. Antoine Twining.

"Rusty!" he cried. "Thank heavens you're here. I've got to talk to you!"

He didn't even look mad.

Just frightened.

21. Dr. Twining

"I had a feeling you were going to figure this out before the was over," said Dr. Twining.

He was sitting on one of the lab stools, next to the large treatment table I had helped him bring over to the colony earlier that afternoon. His coffee maker was sitting on top of the table, and he had just poured himself a cup of coffee — his seventh or eight of the evening if the level in the carafe was any indicator.

He asked if we wanted a cup.

"We'll pass," I said, answering for both of us. I wasn't taking any chances.

He looked sad. "I'm not that kind, Rusty," he said. "I hoped you would understand that."

"I do," I said. "I think. But at this point I'm still figuring better safe than sorry."

Cassie looked from Twining to me, totally mystified.

"Don't worry," I said to her. "It'll all be clear soon enough."

"How did you figure it out?" asked Dr. Twining.

I shrugged. "A little bit of this, a little bit of that. It was the hands that finally put it all together for me. They were all wrong."

I heard Cassie gasp. I wondered how much she had just figured out.

Dr. Twining sighed. "I was afraid of that. I could have taken care of that, if it hadn't been such a rush job."

He straightened his long frame. "Not that I would have wanted to. That's why I'm so glad you're here. This has gone on long enough. It has to come to a stop. Now. Tonight. Before something worse happens." He hesitated, then added: "Some of the others are involved with things that are downright dangerous."

"Dr. Durkin?" I said, making a guess.

Dr. Twining nodded. "Someone has to stop him before it's too late. If it's not too late already." He rose from his chair and began pacing back and forth in front of us. "It's a very confusing issue. I'm in this mess now because I just couldn't give up on some questions. Yet I feel strongly that Pieter has to do what I wouldn't. He's got to give up his research. It's just too dangerous."

The first guess had worked. I thought I would try another. "That's what you two were arguing about the other day," I said.

He nodded. "Certainly. Of course, the whole thing is really her fault, when you come right down to it."

"Her?" I said, suddenly mystified.

Dr. Twining shrugged. "Well, if you go way back, you could put the blame on the company, I guess. They should know you can't put limits on research, can't tell people 'you can only learn this much and no more.' But she was the one who took advantage of the situation."

It wasn't like Dr. Twining to be so obscure. I decided it was a combination of the caffeine buzz he had given himself and the emotional strain he had been under.

That didn't make things any more clear though. A minute ago I thought I had the whole thing figured out. Now my head was starting to spin again. "Wait a minute," I said desperately. "You're getting ahead of me. What 'she' are we talking about?"

Dr. Twining actually stopped pacing and smiled. "You still haven't finished the puzzle, have you, Rusty? You've got method, but not the motive."

He rubbed his hands over his face, as if by that gesture he could wipe away some of his nervousness, his exhaustion, his guilt.

"It's very simple, really. We wanted to work. She made it possible."

"Who?" I asked again.

"Her!" he said, more loudly. He sounded terrified this time, and for an instant I wondered if he was losing his mind.

By the time I realized he was actually pointing at someone behind me, it was too late. Dr. Twining had gasped in shock and begun to slump forward.

Time seems to slow down in a situation like that, maybe because you play it over and over again in your head later on, so that all the little details you normally miss become achingly clear. Even now I can remember the way his mouth opened and closed on the way down, as if he was trying to think of what to say next . . . the way the top of his head looked as it struck the treatment table . . . even the way the coffee pot arced slowly though the air when his arm sent it sliding off the table and onto the floor.

But most of all I remember the sight of the red stain that was already starting to spread around the small, clean hole where the laser had sizzled out through the back of his lab coat.

I spun around. But the door, which had opened while we were talking, had closed again.

I looked back toward my mentor. A ten-pound stone seemed to have found its way into my throat in the instant that had passed since his last words.

Cassie was already at his side, kneeling over him, to see what could be done.

What could be done was nothing, of course.

Once she realized that, she turned away from the body and stood up. "I hate you," she said.

For once I was smart enough to realize that what one was saying was not necessarily what one meant.

I walked over to her and put my arms around her.

She buried her face against my chest and began to cry. I felt like crying too.

I could feel her trembling.

"I'm frightened," she said.

If she was only frightened she was ahead of me. I was downright terrified. And horrified. But it didn't seem like the time to say so.

I held her for just an instant longer than was really necessary. "Can you pull yourself together?" I asked. "We've got work to do here."

She pulled away from me. "Here? Are you crazy? We have to get out of here! Three people are dead already. Do you want to be the fourth?"

"Second," I said.

"What do you mean?"

"Second dead person," I said. "So far poor Dr. Twining is the only person who's actually died."

Cassie looked at me as if I were crazy. It was a look I had gotten used to.

"What are you talking about?" she said.

"Dead people. And living ones — which may include Dr. Puckett, if we're both fast and lucky. Now, we can take the time for me to explain all that to you. Or we can look for him, which considering what just happened would be my recommendation. Under the circumstances, I can't guarantee 'she' — whoever she is — is going to keep him alive much longer."

She started to protest, then thought better of it. "Shouldn't we call someone?" she asked, glancing over at Dr. Twining's body.

"You can try," I said. "But I doubt it will go through."

She went to the console and tapped out a number.

The line was as dead as Dr. Twining.

We were on our own.

"All right," she said. "What do we do now?"

I had just been asking myself the same question. We had come over here looking for information. Now I had a real murder and more new questions than I knew what to do with. I was scrambling desperately to try to put them all together.

"Let's start with Dr. Twining's private office," I said.

"Start what?"

"The search."

"What are we looking for?"

"Any clue to where they might be holding Dr. Puckett." I paused, then added, "But don't restrict yourself to clues. If you get lucky, you might just skip the clues and find the man."

She looked at me sideways, still unwilling to believe what she knew I was telling her. I understood her reluctance, especially under the circumstances. It would be too much to bear if she let herself hope that Dr. Puckett was still alive and then found out that he wasn't. It would be like losing him twice.

I didn't give her a chance to question me; I moved into the office and started tearing it apart.

It wasn't going to be easy. Dr. Twining was hardly what you would call a born criminal. But he was more than bright enough to cover his tracks when he wanted to.

I had been in his private office three or four times before, mostly when he wanted to have some conference about my work. The basic layout was pretty much the same as Dr. Durkin's. I figured that was probably true of all seven of the major labs in the BS Factory. Professional jealousy made it unlikely that anyone would have an office significantly better — or even significantly different — from anyone else's. The major way in which Dr. Twining's differed from Dr. Durkin's was in the furnishings, which were considerably more sparse; but then Dr. Twining never had demonstrated much of a taste for luxury. Aside from the desk and computer, his room held a large table, littered with personal papers and several months worth of magazines and journals; a battered purple easy chair; and a long, comfortable looking sofa, where I had a feeling he often spent the night. Notes and diagrams relating to his work covered the walls.

"Check the bathroom," I said to Cassie as she came into the room behind me. I was already going through Dr. Twining's desk.

I've heard my grandfather complain that going through people's desks isn't what it used to be. There was a time when you could count on a person keeping most of their important papers in their desk. Now the good stuff is usually locked up inside their computer.

That seemed to be the case with Dr. Twining. Nothing I could find in his desk seemed to mean anything.

"Nothing in there," said Cassie, coming out of the bathroom. "What's behind that door?"

She was pointing to a door in the back of the room, in about the same location as the one I had seen Dr. Durkin use earlier that day when I was hiding in his office.

I didn't know.

"Shall I try it?" she asked.

I hesitated. The problem with the doors in this place is that you can't open them just a crack and peek through. You push a button, they slide into the wall, and there you are, completely exposed to whoever is on the other side.

It's enough to give a snoop a nervous breakdown.

"Is there an intercom?" I asked. "Any way we might be able to check on what's on the other side?"

She searched the frame.

"Got it," she said.

She pushed a button, then pulled her hand away as if she had been burned.

I didn't blame her.

I had been hoping we would be able to tell if there was anyone on the other side of the door; maybe pick up voices, or even a conversation.

What we got was an angry babble of people shouting.

That, and the most blood-curdling scream I had ever heard.

22. Air Ducts

When I heard that scream, I did what I generally do: I acted first and thought later.

It was simple, really. Someone was in trouble. When someone's in trouble, you help. That's what I was always taught; that's what MacDonald of Terra always did.

Except he was usually a little brighter about it than I am.

But really, I couldn't help myself. When that scream came roaring through the intercom, it seemed like there was only one thing to do.

I did it. Dashing past Cassie, I jabbed the "Open" button at the side of the door. Then I stood there waiting for it to slide into the wall so I could rush through and help whoever was in trouble.

Fortunately for the White Knight of the BS Factory, the door was locked. Nothing happened.

"Nice work, boy wonder," said Cassie. "Are you sure you're not secretly harboring some kind of death wish?"

"Someone's in trouble!" I said, still not thinking entirely clearly.

"I can think of at least three people who are in trouble," she said. "And two of them are you and me."

She had a point.

"Maybe we should take this a little more slowly," I said.

"Your brilliance outshines the sun," she replied.

I walked back to Dr. Twining's desk. "We've got to find out what's on the other side of that door anyway," I said, tapping a command into his computer. "There's one like it in Dr. Durkin's office, too. Probably one in all the offices. I don't know where they lead. Could be anything back there."

The machine began to beep. "Access denied," read the screen.

I stood up and headed for the lab. "Come on," I said to Cassie. "And bring your magic card with you."

The computer in Dr. Twining's office was for his use only, as were most of the computers in the lab. They operated strictly on passwords. But each lab had at least one computer that could be accessed by means of an I.D. card.

I headed for ours.

"Log on," I said to Cassie, standing aside and gesturing toward the seat.

She did. The computer acknowledged her existence and the extremely high level of her access code.

"What do you want me to look for?" she said.

"The plans for this deathtrap," I said. "I want to know what's behind that wall and if there's anyway we can get there."

She furrowed her brow and tapped in a command. It brought up some generally useless information. She tried again. We got a twenty-item menu that looked like it might possibly lead us where we wanted to go.

Tracking down something like this on a computer can be like trying to find a specific apple on a tree. You start out on the trunk. As soon as it starts to branch, you have to make a choice about which way to go. Using whatever clues you've got, you take the path that makes the most sense. More branches, more choices. Maybe you make six different choices before you get to the end of a branch. If when you get there you find the wrong apple, which is to say if you've taken the wrong path, you go back and start again.

Sometimes you go back just a few branches; sometimes you have to go all the way back to the trunk.

That was basically the process we were following now. It's a good thing the computer was relatively fast. Otherwise I might have gone out of my mind before we found the path that led us to something useful. More than once I wanted to push Cassie aside and attack the keyboard myself, though I knew that wouldn't really speed things up any.

"Air ducts!" I shouted, as she pulled up another submenu. "Try the air ducts!"

It was just what we needed. With a tap of a key she called up a map of the air-duct system for the entire BS Factory.

"Pull up the specs," I said eagerly.

She did. We were in luck. About half of the system was large enough to crawl through.

I don't know how long we spent going over the system. With the memory of that scream echoing in my head, it seemed like hours. In reality, I doubt it was even ten minutes.

The computer was being very obliging about showing us close-ups and cutaway sections. What it wouldn't do was provide an accurate label of what was behind Dr. Twining's wall, even when we found a clear diagram of the complete BS Factory. Most of what the diagram showed I already knew. The bulk of the facility was divided among the seven major labs, which formed a circle around the perimeter of the station. Other areas were set aside for storage, for meetings, even guest rooms where visiting officials could spend the night if they wanted.

All these were clearly marked.

But the central area, which could be accessed from all seven labs, and which I had never seen before, was labeled Storage.

I didn't believe it for a minute. That area was being used for something besides storage.

Even Cassie the cynic thought that must be the case.

When we finally had a good sense of the system, we had the computer print out a couple of maps for us.

Then we returned to Dr. Twining's office. "There," I said, pointing to the wall opposite his desk.

The air vent, which was located near the ceiling, was easily two feet on each side. Climbing into it would be no problem at all, if we could just get the baffle off.

That was a fairly big if. Depending on the construction techniques that had been used, it might be held on with nothing but snaps, or it might be bolted in with fasteners that required a special tool to undo.

I was hoping for the former.

With Cassie's help I moved the large treatment table underneath the vent. In the low gravity, it was easy to climb up on the thing without straining my bum hip.

I stuck my fingers through the grating and pulled. Nothing happened.

Flexing my arms, I pulled myself up so that I could look through the vent. I was light enough that I could almost have held myself straight out from the wall if I wanted.

The vent was locked in place by simple bracket fasteners, one at each corner. I put my fingers through and twisted them.

Once they were loosened the vent slipped out as easily as a watermelon seed slips between your fingers.

I looked down at Cassie.

"You coming?" I said. "Or would you rather stay here?"

She looked around at the office and through the door to where Dr. Twining's body lay in a pool of blood. She climbed up on the table beside me.

"You're better than no company at all," she said curtly.

I hoisted myself up and into the air shaft. Her sharp words would have bothered me, except that I chalked them up to fear. That and the fact that I knew she was being driven crazy by the same question that was ripping at me: who had we heard screaming?

Or, to be more specific: had that scream come from Dr. Elmo Puckett?

23. Dr. Durkin

It was the corners that were killing me. Every time I had to go around one it twisted my hip in a way that made it feel like it was going to come out of my body.

The rest of the trip wasn't that bad, at least not till we got close to the end. The plastic air ducts were clean, and large enough for us to move fairly rapidly. The low gravity helped, of course. Instead of crawling along on our bellies like you normally would in a situation like that, we were able to do a kind of fingertip walk that positioned our bodies in the center of the ducts and let us move through them while barely touching them.

Except for the corners. But after we turned the second one, I didn't feel so bad for myself. We could hear the screaming again, somewhere up ahead of us. Whatever was going on up there, someone was experiencing pain that made what I was suffering seem insignificant.

"Do you hear it?" hissed Cassie, a few seconds after we had rounded that second corner.

I did a kind of pushup, pressing my entire body against the top of the duct. This let me look back underneath myself so that I could see her.

"I hear it," I whispered, as softly as I could. Then I held a finger to my lips to caution her against any more talking. I didn't know how far the sound would carry through these things.

We came to a branch in the ducts. I took out the map to see if I could figure out which way we should go, then decided I didn't need it. All I had to do was listen. The screamer would be my guide.

Or would have been, except that, as it turned out, the duct leading most directly to the sound was one of the ones that narrowed down as it approached the room. That would have been clear enough if I had stuck with the map, instead of being so confident about following the sound of the scream.

By the time we had traveled about thirty feet along the smooth plastic tube it became clear anyway. I simply couldn't go any further. I had felt the duct narrowing around me, of course. But I had just assumed that I was going to be able to make it to the end.

Wrong.

My shoulders jammed in the tube, and I just couldn't go any further. My hip was starting to throb. And the screaming, which still hadn't let up, was beating around my ears.

The only good thing about the whole mess was that with the amount of noise coming into the duct, I figured no one would notice a little coming out of it. I scuffled around and pushed myself backward.

I heard a muffled sound from behind me. I had run into Cassie.

She grabbed my leg and gave it a yank, to warn me to slow down.

Generally, foolish pride has kept me from telling people about my hip. But when that lightning bolt of pain shot up my leg and through my skull I did two things. First I bit my thumb, to keep from screaming. And second, I promised myself not to be so secretive in the future. Pride has its price, but this was ridiculous.

We backed slowly down the tunnel. If I thought making the corners had been a problem when we were going forward, I should have reserved judgment until I had a chance to try it backward. Just the memory of it makes my leg twitch.

I would have given almost anything to be able to turn around and go forward. But the very thought of trying it made the duct seem twice as narrow as it really was.

A hiss from behind indicated that Cassie wanted to talk to me.

For a glorious instant I thought maybe I should push myself against the wall and let her work her way up so that we were face to face. It would be delightfully cozy. But we had work to do, and we might get stuck that way. I could think of worse ways to die, but I wasn't ready to cash in my chips for the sake of a good snuggle yet.

"What now?" she hissed.

I pressed a finger to my lips. Then I took out the map and waved it at her, so she would know that I was trying to solve the problem. I knew it could be maddening to be trapped in these ducts and think you were going nowhere.

The solution was fairly simple in print, though I could tell it was going to be hard on my hip. We had to go forward about thirty meters, then make a sharp turn that would take us back in the direction we wanted to go.

I folded up the map and started moving.

The corner was worse than I expected. The fact that once I had managed to get my head and shoulders around it I could hear the screaming again didn't help matters any.

Though she didn't make a sound, I could sense Cassie's impatience. I pulled myself forward, trying to ignore the fire in my hip.

I could see a square of light that marked the end of the duct.

I pulled myself forward.

I wished I hadn't.

The scene in the space ahead of me was like something out of a nightmare. Five upright tanks stood at the right side of the room. Four of them held exact duplicates of Hank Smollin. A maze of wires and tubes ran from each tank to a console about ten feet away.

That was the good part. Bizarre as it was, at least it verified my theory.

Much worse was the glass cage in the center of the room.

Inside its unbreakable walls, Pieter Durkin

was flinging himself from side to side, screaming in rage and fright. He was bleeding from
at least a dozen places and his pale blond hair
was matted with blood. As I watched him tear
at his own arms and legs I realized that his
wounds were self-inflicted.

Standing in front of the cage were three of
the remaining "Mad Scientists" of the BS
Factory. I recognized the short, stocky figure of
Martha Collins, the tall, distinguished looking
Charles Hulan, and the even taller Virginia
Jefferson.

Dr. Collins was the first to speak after I
reached the vent.

"I think we should kill him now and get it
over with," she said.

I'm surprised they didn't hear my gasp of
shock, even over Dr. Durkin's screams.

I started to undo the fasteners at the corners
of the vent (a task which was considerably
easier from the inside than it had been from the
outside). I wasn't sure what I was going to do
once I had the thing off. I just wanted to be
ready in case I figured something out.

As it turned out, the situation was taken out
of my hands. I had just loosened the fourth
fastener. Bracing my hands against the floor of
the duct, I pulled myself forward as far as possible, in order to hear what Dr. Jefferson was
saying in her low, competent voice. It was about
then that Cassie got impatient.

She gave my leg a tug, to remind me she was
still here.

It was the last straw for my hip. I felt like

someone had poured liquid fire into the socket. Bellowing in pain, I involuntarily stiffened my arms. The action caused me to shoot forward. My face smashed against the vent. With the clips undone, it easily gave way.

The next thing I knew, I was laying on the floor, looking up at three very surprised, very angry scientists.

24. Forbidden Research

For a moment we all just kind of looked at each other.

Dr. Collins was the first to speak.

"What are *you* doing here?" she said.

I wanted desperately to come up with some sizzling rejoinder. But it was hard to think with a lump of fire where my hip should be and Dr. Durkin gibbering and screaming like a madman while he slammed himself against the glass walls of his cage. I settled for moral outrage.

"Why don't you help him?" I cried.

"Don't you think we would if we could?" said Dr. Jefferson. She reached down to help me up. But as soon as she let go of my arm my hip gave way and I crumpled to the floor again. She put her hand out to me again, but I waved her off. "Never mind," I gasped. "It'll be better in a while."

To say I was confused would be putting it mildly. I thought I had finally found the villains of the situation. But all three of these people gave evidence of being genuinely concerned about what was happening to Dr. Durkin.

I nodded toward the cage. "What's going on?" I asked.

The scientists exchanged glances. "He might as well be told," said Dr. Hulan. "He knows this much, and the whole thing is coming unraveled anyway. There's not much point in covering up now, because no matter what we do, it won't stay covered."

Dr. Collins sighed. "I think you're right, Charles," she said. "The game is over."

"Some game," I said, glancing at Dr. Durkin.

Hulan shuddered. "Cruel as it is to say, Pieter brought that on himself. The rest of us tried to tell him that he wasn't taking sufficient precautions. Of course, that's part of the problem when you're doing research under these conditions. . . ."

"What conditions?" I said "This is one of the most advanced research facilities in the world!"

"Certainly it is," said Dr. Collins. "For approved projects. But if you want to work at the real cutting edge of things, if you want to push toward something beyond what those bureaucratic imbeciles that license these facilities are willing to approve, then you end up cutting some corners."

"You were *all* doing bootleg research!" I said in surprise. "I thought it was just Dr. Twining."

I had figured out what Dr. Twining was up to when I realized what had bothered me about Dr. Puckett's hands. But even then it hadn't occurred to me that the entire senior staff of the BS Factory would be up to their necks in the stuff.

"Not all of us," said Dr. Collins. "Dr. Gomiri kept her nose clean. Virginia, here, did, too. The only reason she's here now is because I asked her to help us. Considering the number of times she's tried to warn us about something like this, it was pretty big of her to come."

I turned to Dr. Jefferson. "If you're here to help, why don't you?" I demanded. I glanced at Dr. Durkin and shuddered. "Who put him in that cage, anyway?"

"He put himself in," said Dr. Hulan. "As soon as he knew he'd been infected. We can't anaesthetize him because the last two times we tried it, the victim died instantly."

I wondered who the last two victims had been.

Dr. Hulan continued his explanation. "And we can't take him out because we don't know how contagious he is right now. That cage is completely sealed. If we're lucky, what he has will stay in there with him. On the other hand, it's entirely possible this room is already contaminated — which would mean that all of us, including you, my brash young friend, could end up like that."

I shuddered.

"Don't be unnecessarily cruel, Charles," said Dr. Collins.

Hulan shrugged. "It's true, and you know it."

"It's possible. But so far as we know right now, the thing is only transmitted by direct contact with the bloodstream."

I remembered the scene in Dr. Durkin's lab that morning.

"He's got what Ron had!" I said. "Ron and Nancy were the last two victims!"

"Brilliant deduction," said Dr. Hulan acidly.

I remembered that he had participated in the fight. I didn't think he had been scratched. Even so, I could imagine that he was pretty nervous about now. I would have been, in his situation. Now I understood why they had been so adamant about getting Cassie and me out of the room!

"Just what is it he's got?" I asked.

Dr. Jefferson shrugged. "Who knows? He only invented it a few days ago."

"He was doing recombinant DNA!" I cried. This time I was truly shocked. That kind of research had been completely banned after the Chicago disaster that had killed 20,000 people a few years ago.

Dr. Collins nodded. "The ironic thing is, he wasn't even doing anything big, like cancer research. He was just looking for a cure for the common cold. Instead he came up with this."

I hoped Cassie was still in the duct, listening to this. I didn't know how everything was going to turn out. But I had a feeling that if I lived through it, I was going to need a witness.

The only thing still puzzling me was who had killed Dr. Twining? And why? I had assumed it was because he was about to spill the beans about what was going on. But these three were talking about it very openly. Which must mean it wasn't one of them.

But if not them, who?

Suddenly I thought I had an answer.

"What were you doing with your results?" I asked.

Dr. Collins and Dr. Hulan looked at each other nervously.

"They were selling them to me," said a familiar voice. "For a tidy profit, I might add."

I sighed. I had hoped I was mistaken.

But really, it was the most logical answer. We had always joked that she was the one who really ran the BS Factory. And of course, as much as I had tried to ignore the fact, no one had been in a better position to sabotage my scooter.

Gramps always told me that letting personal feelings interfere with your detective work can be a fatal error.

Turning to face my old buddy, Millicent Carter, I hoped Gramps was wrong — at least about the fatal part.

25. Millie

"It's unfortunate you don't think as badly as you drive, Rusty," said Millie. "If you did, you might never have gotten into this mess."

I shrugged. "If it hadn't been me, it would have been someone else. You couldn't have kept this hidden forever. Your trail was getting wider and wider."

Dr. Hulan decided to interrupt. "What's the point of the gun, Millie?" he asked. "You don't need to be that worried. Except for poor Pieter here, nobody's done anything that's going to merit more than a slap on the wrist, and that includes you."

"Tell that to Dr. Twining," I said.

"What do you mean?" asked Dr. Collins.

"I mean Millie has already used that laser pistol once tonight, when Dr. Twining was about to spill the deal to me."

Dr. Collins caught her breath. "Is he dead?" she asked.

"Of course he's dead," snapped Millie. "Rusty and that stupid girl would be, too, if I hadn't been thinking I could get things back under control before they reached this point. Just shows you what I get for being sentimental."

Dr. Durkin, who had been quiet for a while, screamed and began scrabbling at the glass of his isolation cage again.

I wondered what Cassie was doing.

"Why, Millie?" asked Dr. Jefferson.

Millie shrugged. "Because some of us were indeed doing things for which we could have gotten more than a slap on the wrist. You fools thought I was passing your research on to a major corporation. Actually, I was. But they weren't the only ones getting it. The big money was coming from the South American bloc." She smiled. "They had interesting plans for some of the information you people were generating."

Dr. Hulan's face went red. "You betrayed us!" he said.

Millie laughed. "You're as naive as the kid," she said. "Worse, since you've been around long enough to know better."

"Well, you won't get away with it," said Dr. Hulan gruffly.

"Oh, no?" asked Millie. "Who's going to stop me?"

"The four of us, to begin with."

I thought it was nice of Dr. Hulan to count me in. Unfortunately, it didn't seem to make any difference.

"You can't stop me if you're dead," said Millie. "Which you will be, the minute you decide to move. I've already killed one person today. Three or four more aren't going to make that much difference."

"Don't be ridiculous," said Dr. Jefferson, who appeared just as cool as ever. "You can't get away with killing all four of us!"

"Sure I can," said Millie, "If this station happens to blow up sometime after I head back toward the colony. Which it's going to do, by the way. And you're not going to try to stop me, either."

"And why is that?" asked Dr. Collins.

She reached into her coveralls and pulled out a small radio device.

"The minute one of you makes a move toward me, I push this button. When I do, it will set off a small charge that will release three liters of contaminated blood into ICE-3's water supply. Not enough to even affect the taste. But enough to give every person in the place the same thing Durkin has."

She nodded toward the bloody, gibbering creature in the glass cage; he had stopped screaming and was huddled in a corner, trembling and weeping. I couldn't look. It made me sick.

"You're bluffing," said Dr. Hulan. "Even if you're not, it will never work. The disease doesn't spread that way."

"Are you sure?" asked Millie. "Sure enough to bet the lives of 25,000 people?"

"You're crazy," said Dr. Collins.

Millie shrugged. "Could be. I prefer to think that I'm just amoral. And don't count on your girlfriend helping out, either, Rusty," she said, turning toward where I lay on the floor. "I don't know where she is, but there's no way she can either fly out of here or call back to the colony. This place is locked up tight as a drum." She waved her gun at me. "And for heaven's sake, stand up!"

"I'll just fall back down," I said.

"I said, stand up!"

I stood up. I fell down.

"See?" I said.

You might have noticed that these were the first things I had said in some time. That's because I had been busy thinking. Dr. Hulan's comment that no one had done anything serious enough for major punishment indicated to me that none of the scientists knew what had really happened to Dr. Puckett. That confused me, since I had expected to finish off that part of the problem when we got into this room.

So — if he wasn't here, he had to be somewhere else.

But where?

I thought back over everything that had happened in the last few hours.

Suddenly the whole thing fell into place. If my hip hadn't been in such bad shape, I would have kicked myself!

"Where's Dr. Puckett?" I asked.

Millie laughed. "Wouldn't you like to know?" she said.

Actually, I did know. At least, I thought I did. What I was really looking for was a way to get the information to Cassie. I wasn't sure it would do any good. But it seemed to be our only hope.

"What do you mean?" asked Dr. Hulan. "Puckett's dead, isn't he?"

"Is he?" I asked.

Millie laughed again.

"Or is he just getting the treatment?" I asked, emphasizing the last word slightly. "Oh, oh. Table that. Even if we could find him, Millie doesn't like this line of conversation." Again, I emphasized the important words.

Millie looked at me like I was losing my mind. "Shut up, Rusty," she said.

I shut. Either Cassie had the message, or she didn't. Even if she did, I wasn't sure how much good it would do. But I was fresh out of ideas.

The only thing left to do now was stall.

Unfortunately, that wasn't going to be easy, since Millie wanted to get things moving.

She waved her gun at Dr. Jefferson. "You — get something to tie the other ones up with."

I gained new respect for Millie's self-control, since Dr. Jefferson gave her a look that should have split a stone in two. Even so, she went to the back of the room and found some cord. Then, following Millie's directions, she used it to tie Dr. Hulan and Dr. Collins together.

I had read enough of my grandfather's books to know that this was the point where the villain was supposed to take time out to explain how clever he or she is. But Millie had already made it clear she wasn't going to talk about what had happened with Dr. Puckett. I decided to try another angle.

"I don't get one thing," I said. "How did you

get all these bright people involved in this mess anyway?"

"Shut up, Rusty," said Millie, "or I'll blow your head off."

So much for Plan A.

I decided to throw a fit instead. I waited for a minute while Dr. Jefferson finished tying up Hulan and Collins. I waited a bit longer while Millie looked at the two of us, trying to decide just how she was going to finish the job. Then I cut loose.

Thrusting my leg straight out, I began screaming as if someone was trying to cut it off.

"What's he doing?" demanded Millie.

"His leg must have gone into spasm," said Dr. Jefferson. "I'm not surprised, considering the way it's been abused tonight."

That was a relief. If Dr. Jefferson could recognize the symptoms it must mean I was doing a creditable job of imitating a problem my doctor had warned me I might have at some point.

"How long is it going to last?" asked Millie.

Dr. Jefferson shrugged. "A minute or two. He won't be worth much for a while when it's done. They're pretty draining."

That was good news. It ought to put Millie off her guard.

I lay there on the floor, screaming and twitching, my face contorted with pain. Considering the shape I was in, it wasn't much of an acting job. I just showed what I had been feeling.

When I thought I had milked it as long as I

could, I let my body slump and lay there gasping for breath.

Millie came and stood over me. "Is he done now?" she asked.

Dr. Jefferson shrugged again. "It's his leg," she said.

Just then Dr. Durkin leaped to his feet with a blood curdling scream, the worst he had let out yet.

It was all the distraction I needed. I pushed my body backward, thrusting my right leg between Millie's outspread feet. Then I closed my legs like a pair of scissors and threw myself sideways as hard as I could.

That was when all hell broke loose. Dr. Durkin was still screaming. I was, too. Only this time it was for real; the pain from that little maneuver made everything I had suffered so far tonight seem like minor pinpricks by comparison.

Millie was also screaming, but in her case it was with anger instead of pain. Both her gun and the little radio device had gone flying out of her hands when she hit the floor. Now she was scrambling after them. So was Dr. Jefferson, and it was only seconds before the two women were rolling around on the floor having a spectacular fist fight.

The radio device was about twenty feet from me. I began pulling myself across the floor with my hands, hoping I could reach it before Millie did.

It was going to be close. Breaking free from Dr. Jefferson, Millie lunged in my direction. I was too terrified to grab the device, because I knew she would fight me for it, and I was afraid we might accidentally set it off. So I gave it a sideswipe with my hand and sent it skittering across the floor.

Blind with rage, Millie aimed a vicious kick at my hip. It connected, and I condensed into a ball of pain. She spun back toward Dr. Jefferson, who had just retrieved the gun. It was clear that Millie had been trained in the martial arts, because she now lashed out with a pair of kicks that moved so fast I could barely see them. The first knocked the gun out of Dr. Jefferson's hand. The second just plain knocked the scientist senseless.

It looked like it was all over. Hulan and Collins were tied up. Dr. Jefferson was out cold. And I was immobilized with pain.

I started after Millie anyway.

As it turned out, I needn't have bothered. Just as she turned to pick up the gun the door slid open and an eighth of a ton of angry Puckett came flying into the room, waving an old fashioned monkey wrench over his head as though it was King Arthur's sword.

Millie spun around, but it was too late. The wrench connected with her head, and she crumpled in a heap at Dr. Puckett's feet.

"Foolish woman!" he crowed triumphantly. "She should have known better than to mess with Elmo Puckett and his friends!"

I remember being impressed that he had bothered to mention the rest of us.

Then I passed out.

26. The Last Details

The next time I saw that wrench it was mounted in a kind of frame in Dr. Puckett's office. Underneath it was a label, which read:

WENCH WRENCH:
Once used by the heroic Elmo Puckett
to knock Millicent Carter
into the middle of next Tuesday.

The heroic Dr. Puckett himself was floating behind his desk, beaming from ear to ear. He sighed contentedly. "All in all, that was the most fun I've had in years," he said.

"Maybe we should bring in a band of armed guerillas and stage a political takeover for your birthday," said Helen.

"Would you?" he asked, his voice all sweetness and light. "I think I'd like that."

"What I'd like is some answers," said Cassie, "which is what you promised when you set up this meeting!"

"Fire away," said Dr. Puckett. "Though I

may defer some questions to Rusty, since he did such an admirable job of figuring this whole mess out to begin with!"

"OK. Let's start with the big one. What the heck happened to you yesterday?"

Dr. Puckett nodded in my direction. "You want to take a stab at that, Rusty?"

"I'll try," I said, clearing my throat, "if you'll help me fill in the hazy spots."

"An unnecessary request if I ever heard one," said Helen. "Your biggest problem will be to keep him from filling in the clear spots."

"Helen," said Dr. Puckett, "I have been unusually magnanimous in offering to let the boy speak. Haven't you ever heard of positive reinforcement? Why don't you encourage me while you can?"

"I stand corrected," she said. "Fire away, Rusty."

"Well, as near as I can figure it out, when Millie found out Dr. Puckett was coming over to the BS Factory, she panicked."

"Naturally," said Dr. Puckett. "She knew it wouldn't take me long to figure things out."

"If you're so smart how come you were almost dead?" asked Helen.

Dr. Puckett folded his hands over his stomach. "Why don't you continue with your story?" he said to me.

"Well, using threats of exposure, she blackmailed Dr. Twining into getting you out of the way for the time being. You were too valuable for her to kill, of course . . ."

"Of course," said Dr. Puckett.

"What Twining didn't know was that she was planning on selling you to the highest bidder."

"According to the statement she gave the authorities she had several countries and a couple of corporations in mind," said Dr. Puckett contentedly. "I wonder how much she could have gotten for me?"

"Probably about a dollar ninety-eight," said Helen. "But she would have cleaned up once they found out what you were really like and wanted her to take you back."

"Anyway," I said, jumping back into the conversation, "the medicine Dr. Twining gave you when you came for your checkup was something he concocted to induce a simulated heart attack. That was the riskiest part of his plan, of course, since there was always the danger that it would have triggered the real thing — not that that wouldn't have suited Millie just fine. But he never really intended to hurt you. Anyway, you left for the colony, he spent the rest of the afternoon preparing for what came next, which mostly meant getting the treatment table ready so he could use it to sneak your clone into the colony and sneak you back out." I shook my head. "I had no idea when I helped him move that thing out of here that you were inside of it!"

"You should have seen him when I opened the thing up this morning!" said Cassie. "Dr. Twining had him trussed up, tied down, and packed in with so much padding he couldn't have made a noise if he had tried. Not that he was very gracious about being rescued."

"Cassie!" cried Dr. Puckett. "You wound me!"

"What were the first words out of your mouth after I untied the gag?" demanded Cassie.

"If I remember correctly they were 'What took so long?'" Dr. Puckett shrugged. "It seemed like an appropriate question under the circumstances."

Helen snorted but decided not to comment.

"I was worried you wouldn't be able to figure out my message about where he was," I said to Cassie.

She laughed. "At first I thought you had lost your mind, shouting about 'treatments' and 'tabling' the idea. Then when you hit the words 'find him' like you did, it suddenly seemed so clear I was afraid Millie would figure out what you were up to. But this is where I get confused. How did you figure out the corpse was a fake to begin with? And why was Dr. Twining making a clone of Elmo anyway?"

Dr. Puckett spread his hands as if the answer was obvious. "Can you think of a better subject?" he asked.

"Actually, I'd be hard pressed to come up with anything more frightening than the thought of having two of you around," said Helen.

"Could someone just answer my questions?" pleaded Cassie.

I spoke fast, before Dr. Puckett had a chance

to come out with another one-liner. "As far as figuring out it was a clone," I said, "the answer was in the hands. Something about them kept bothering me, and when I finally realized what it was, I knew that corpse couldn't be the real thing. Spread out your hands," I said to Dr. Puckett.

He laid them on the desk in front of him. They were indeed as I remembered them.

"The clone was a genetic duplicate of Elmo," I said. "But of course, it wouldn't have any of his acquired characteristics. That was one reason Dr. Twining really roughed the body up when he was pretending to treat it for heart attack. He figured the distress of the treatment would distort the features enough to cover any discrepancies we might notice. But he forgot about this."

I reached out and touched the permanent brown smear that Dr. Puckett's years of nicotine addiction had left between the first and second fingers of the right hand. "The hands of the clone were missing the evidence of your old vice," I said to him.

"Very clever, Rusty. And a potent demonstration of the usefulness of vices. As to why Antoine had cloned me to begin with, the answer is it's because he was a worry-wart. He had convinced himself that I was going to have a heart attack before the year was over, and he was hoping that if he could get a viable duplicate of me, he would have a strong new heart to transplant into my body, a perfect match that would stand no chance of rejection. Of course, as my physician, it was easy enough for him to get the raw material for the cloning. All he really needed was the kind of tissue sample you can take any time you do a physical." A surprisingly wistful smile crossed Dr. Puckett's face. "When you come right down to it, it was pretty thoughtful of Antoine."

"And it was a natural path for his research," I pointed out. "Or would have been, if the government hadn't outlawed human cloning experiments ten years ago. Growing body parts with clones would be the next best thing to actual tissue regeneration. And if he had been successful in your case, he might have been able to reverse the government's ruling on the matter."

"OK," said Helen, "so Dr. Twining was making clones, and Dr. Durkin, rest his soul, was fiddling around with DNA. But what got this whole thing started was the body that Rusty saw in the waste treatment facility. Since there were four more just like it at the BS Factory, I assume it was a clone of Hank Smollin. But why was it in the trash?"

"There you've got me," I said. "I have no idea."

"I do," said Dr. Puckett. "I picked it up from conversations between Antoine and Millie that I overheard while I was locked up in that treatment table. It seems Antoine had used a tissue sample he took from Smollin to make several experimental clones. He had one of them out in his lab when he got an unexpected visit from one of the colony's political hot-shots. If they had caught him working on an essentially dead body, there would have been an uproar. So he dumped it in his waste system, planning on retrieving it later. But the official overstayed his welcome, and by the time Antoine got back to it, the thing had been collected with the rest of the waste materials. Since it's pretty much a closed system, he figured that would be the end of it." Dr. Puckett glanced in my direction. "He hadn't counted on your bizarre little bit of poking around in the vats to see what was in them. I imagine when he got word that you had found the body he just about went out of his skin."

"A potent demonstration of the usefulness of vices," I said smugly.

27. The Stars

I adjusted the parameters on the radio-telescope and leaned back in my seat.

"Very good, Rusty," said Dr. Puckett. "Give me ten or twelve years, and I'll make a scientist out of you yet."

I sighed. Having Dr. Puckett as a mentor wasn't going to be easy. I would learn a lot. But I was certainly going to pay a heavy price for it.

"Have you got your speech ready?" he asked me now.

I nodded.

Memorial services for Dr. Twining and Dr. Durkin were scheduled for that afternoon; as Dr. Twining's former protégé, I was expected to speak.

The thought had frightened me at first. I've never liked talking in front of people, though by the time I was done testifying at Millie's trial, I was pretty used to it.

What changed my mind was when I finally figured out I had something I *needed* to say about Dr. Twining. Not about the man himself — other people would be doing that. But I wanted to talk a little about his work, which I thought was important, and the fact that he might still be alive if he hadn't been driven into secrecy to pursue the scientific questions that burned inside of him.

Dr. Puckett and my grandfather had both helped me put together my speech. Dr. Puckett was especially excited, because he had slipped in a few particularly outrageous comments and couldn't wait to hear me deliver them.

I cut a couple of them out without telling him. But a few more were right on target, and I intended to zing them out there. Elmo was convinced they would make the international news.

I stared at the image on the wall screen. It showed a star cluster about 48 trillion miles away.

We would be launching the bodies of Dr. Twining and Dr. Durkin toward it later this afternoon.

It struck me as funny. If we were as scientific and advanced as we liked to believe, we would just recycle Dr. Twining's body for its chemicals.

But like Dr. Durkin, whose body was contaminated anyway, he was to be buried in space.

I thought about the long journey they were about to begin.

It was the same one I wanted to make, though I hoped I would still be alive when I started it.

I had been talking to Cassie. To my surprise, she had the same dream, that someday she would be on the first ship we sent to the stars.

She and Helen would be at the memorial service that afternoon — "for moral support," as they phrased it.

Afterward, Cassie and I were going out for a bite to eat.

All in all, the afternoon looked like it might be fairly interesting.

For that matter, so did the next forty or fifty years.